"What in the name of ground beef . . . ?"

Dexter dipped a French fry into Ed's sauce, then shoved it into his boss's mouth.

Mr. Baily started to protest . . . but then he began to chew. His lips smacked loudly, and his eyes grew wider and wider. His mouth spread into a grin as he said, "This is . . . *marvelous!* Where did this sauce *come* from?"

"Ed made it himself!" Dexter said happily.

"This is *excellent!*" Monique exclaimed.

"It's *awesome!*" Deedee declared.

Smacking his lips, Otis looked at Mr. Baily with a half smile and said, "It makes me glad I'm not dead."

Dexter pulled Ed from the booth and asked, "Do you realize what'll happen if we start puttin' this stuff on Good Burgers?"

Ed stared at him for a moment, then replied, "They'll get all covered with sauce?"

"No!" Dexter replied. "Well, yeah, but . . . just *listen,* okay? If we put that sauce on Good Burgers, everyone'll wanna *eat* here! We'll knock Mondo Burger off the *map!*"

Look for these Nickelodeon® books:

The Secret World of Alex Mack™
Are You Afraid of the Dark?®
The Mystery Files of Shelby Woo™
Clarissa Explains It All®: Boys
The Big Help™ Book
Good Burger™

Available from MINSTREL Books

GOOD BURGER™

A NOVELIZATION BY JOSEPH LOCKE
BASED ON THE SCREENPLAY BY
DAN SCHNEIDER AND KEVIN KOPELOW & HEATH SEIFERT

A
MINSTREL®
BOOK

Published by POCKET BOOKS
New York   London   Toronto   Sydney   Tokyo   Singapore

A MINSTREL PAPERBACK *Original*

 A Minstrel Book published by
POCKET BOOKS, a division of Simon & Schuster Inc.
1230 Avenue of the Americas, New York, NY 10020

ISBN: 0-671-01692-X

First Minstrel Books printing August 1997

10 9 8 7 6

Photography by Mark Fellman, Robert Isenberg, and Charlie Pizzarello

Printed in the U.S.A.

Dedicated to
Lisa Clancy
Liz Shiflett
and
Erica Pass
With thanks!

GOOD BURGER™

Chapter 1

Everything was so normal that Ed had no idea he was dreaming.

He was at work, manning his post behind the counter at Good Burger, the most average burger joint in America. He wore his Good Burger uniform and, on his striped shirt, a name tag that announced proudly, "I'm Ed!" Just another day at work—or so it seemed—with just another customer standing at the counter.

"Excuse me," a woman called. "Hello? Young man?"

Ed turned and faced the woman, saying, "Welcome to Good Burger, home of the Good Burger, can I take your order?"

The woman scanned the menu posted high on the wall behind Ed. "Just a Good Burger, please. And I'd like that to go."

Ed's eyebrows popped up as he stared at the woman. "To go where?"

1

The woman frowned. "To go . . . well, to my *house*."

"Okay," Ed said cheerfully, removing a pad and pen from his pocket. He placed the pad on the counter and prepared to write, asking, "What's your address?"

"My . . . *what?*" Frustrated, she sighed and said firmly, "Look, I just want a Good Burger, okay?"

"Okay, okay," Ed said soothingly. "Easy, Mister."

As Ed turned to the microphone, the woman squinted at him, confused. *"Mister?"*

"One Good Burger," Ed said into the microphone.

Yes, it was just another normal day at work, so far . . . at least, until Ed turned around and faced the neatly wrapped Good Burgers lined up beneath the heat lamps. He plucked one of the burgers from the tray and shook open a paper bag. But before he could stuff the burger into the bag, he heard a small, muffled voice.

"No, Ed! *Noooo!*" the voice whined. And it was coming from . . . the *hamburger!*

Ed's mouth dropped open. "What the . . ."

Opening the wrapper, Ed peeked inside at the burger . . . and he was so shocked, he nearly dropped it. The burger stared up at him with great big puppy dog eyes and a happy beef-patty-and-lettuce grin.

"Don't sell me, Ed!" the burger cried in a squeaky voice. "Please? I wanna stay here with you!"

Two more burgers beneath the heat lamps began to wiggle around until their faces were poking out of their wrappers.

"Me, too!" one of the burgers exclaimed.

"We *love* you, Ed!" another cried.

"Whooaaa!" Ed blurted. "I'm hallucin . . . hallu-cin . . . er, uh, hallu . . . I'm *imaginin'* stuff!"

Suddenly, *all* the burgers under the heat lamps poked their faces from their wrappers and grinned up at Ed. The burgers rose from their places on the aluminum tray and began to float around Ed in a grinning swirl of beef patties and sesame seed buns!

"Come with us, Ed!" one of the burgers said.

"Fly, Ed! Fly!"

"Yes, Ed! Fly with us!"

Ed's eyes grew to twice their normal size as his feet left the tile floor and he began to float upward with the chattering, smiling Good Burgers.

"Whooaaa!" Ed exclaimed. "I'm flyin' with fast food!"

Ed continued to rise up in the air, surrounded by the floating hamburgers . . . until a loud, obnoxious buzzer sounded from . . . from . . . well, from *someplace*. The buzzer startled Ed so much that he faltered there in the air . . . and then began to plummet downward, out of control, until—

He sat bolt upright in bed and babbled rapidly, "Wel-come to Good Burger, home of the Good Burger, can I take your—"

Ed realized he was in bed, in his bedroom.

"Whoa," he muttered. "A dream." He turned to his left and focused his bleary eyes on the buzzing alarm clock. It read 9:50 A.M. "Whoa! A clock!" He hit the button and killed the buzzer, then threw his covers aside.

As usual, Ed was already dressed for work because, as

3

usual, he'd slept in his Good Burger uniform. Ed was the kind of guy who liked to simplify his life as much as possible, and one of the ways he did that was to dress for work every night before going to bed. Ed took a great deal of pride in the fact that he was a *very* simple guy.

In the bathroom, Ed turned on the shower and stepped beneath the hot spray. As he lathered up, he sang, "I'm a dude . . . She's a dude . . . He's a dude . . . 'Cause we're all dudes!"

He had already forgotten all about his dream . . . just as he had forgotten to remove his Good Burger uniform before getting into the shower.

There were no talking, flying hamburgers at the *real* Good Burger that day, but there were *plenty* of customers. And they were growing impatient.

Ed was late for work, and the line at the counter was getting longer. All of Ed's coworkers were busily going about their individual jobs. Unfortunately, none of those jobs included waiting on the customers at the counter.

Monique was handling the fries and onion rings. Deedee worked on the fresh vegetables and put together the salads. Spatch was at the grill flipping patties. And Otis . . . well, Otis was around somewhere; he was in his mid-eighties and even when he was at his busiest, he didn't move very quickly.

Fizz was working the drive-through window. He was walking past the front counter with his headset on when an impatient customer barked at him.

4

"Hey, you!" He was a beefy man wearing a construction worker's helmet. "Would you *please* take my order?"

Fizz skidded to a stop and turned to the man with a grin. "No can do!" he replied. "I'm the drive-through guy. You need the counter guy."

The man rolled his eyes. "Well, where *is* the counter guy?"

"I'm not sure," Fizz said. He turned around and asked Monique, "Where's Ed?"

At that moment, Ed was shooting out of his house on a pair of Rollerblades, headed for work at high speed.

Once Ed had realized he was wearing his uniform in the shower, he'd had to change into a dry one, and that had made him late. But there was nothing slow about Ed as he zoomed down the sidewalk on his skates. He quickly realized he was going a little *too* fast as he neared three little girls jumping rope on the sidewalk. He careened back and forth, hoping to avoid them, but it was impossible. Instead, he decided to take the friendly approach.

"Mornin', girls!" he shouted as he closed in on them. He sped between them, getting tangled in the rope. "Whoooaaa!" he cried as he recovered his balance, pawing at the rope that was twined around his body.

"Hey!" one of the girls shouted. She held on to the rope and ran behind him as he picked up speed. "That's our *rope!*"

Ed disentangled himself from the rope and let it go. "My fault!" he called as he raced down the sidewalk. "Happy jumpin'!"

As Ed hurried to Good Burger, the line at the counter was growing longer, and the customers were becoming angry.

The woman standing at the head of the line leaned over the counter, frowning, and looked around. When she spotted Monique, she called, "Excuse me? *Miss?*"

"Yeah, can I help you?" Monique asked, hurrying to the counter.

The woman's face screwed up into a tight, angry expression. "I just wanna order some *food!*"

"Oh, no problem!" Monique said with a smile.

"Good," the woman huffed. *"Finally!"*

"Ed?" Monique called, stepping back from the counter and looking around. "Ed? Hey, *Ed!*"

But Ed wasn't there. He was weaving his way down the street, trying to get to work as fast as possible. That wasn't very fast, though, because Ed wasn't exactly a great in-line skater.

He hopped a curb and zigzagged on the sidewalk, trying to avoid pedestrians. He annoyed a few people, but always called out an apology, or at least a *hello,* over his shoulder as he passed them. But each time he turned his head to call over his shoulder, he took his eyes off where he was going for just a couple seconds. Before he knew it, Ed found himself hurtling toward a woman pushing a baby carriage.

"Whoooaaa!" Ed shouted, flailing his arms as he rapidly closed the distance between himself and the unexpecting mother. "Look out, lady!"

The woman let out a sharp yelp as she plucked her baby from the carriage and took a step backward . . . but it was too late.

Ed slammed into the woman, bounced off her like a pinball, spun around a couple of times, then shot onward down the sidewalk. He turned his head and called over his shoulder, "Sorry!" But when he faced front again, he saw that there was a baby in his arms! "Hey! Baby!" he said with a laugh. "Coochie-coochie-coo!"

The wide-eyed baby smiled and gurgled a giggle at him.

Ed was approaching the corner of the block, but cut through a neighborhood basketball court to save time. All the while, he and the baby grinned and babbled at each other.

On the basketball court, some neighborhood guys were involved in a tough, fast game, so tough and fast that they didn't see Ed coming their way with his accidental passenger.

"Over here!" one of the guys shouted to a teammate. When the other player passed him the ball, he drove in for a layup.

Suddenly, a mass of bodies converged under the basket . . . and Ed slammed into them like a killer meteor!

The basketball players shouted at Ed as he sped away, then looked around for the ball. The player who'd been on his way to a layup tilted his head back and looked up . . . and smiled. He saw something coming down toward him and held out his hands to catch it.

Once out of the basketball court and on the sidewalk again, Ed looked down at the baby.

"Whoooaaa!" he shouted. The baby was gone! He was carrying a basketball!

Back on the court, the guy caught what he *thought* was the basketball, laid it up off the backboard and into the basket.

"Two points!" he shouted.

One of his teammates caught the object as it dropped through the basket and stared at it in shock. It was a baby . . . and the baby looked up at him and giggled.

Looking around at the other stunned players with a confused frown, the guy asked, "Does that *count?*"

In minutes, Good Burger was in sight. Ed whizzed through the parking lot, wobbling and swerving a little.

An old lady with a cane was hobbling toward the front entrance. Her hand was on the handle of the door as Ed closed in quickly.

"Doooor!" he shouted.

The old lady made a sound like a duck and stumbled backward, still clutching at the handle of the door, pulling it open.

"Thank you!" Ed said as he sailed into Good Burger.

"That's *it!*" barked the angry man in the construction worker's helmet at the counter.

Ed glided in and made his way into the back.

"Five more seconds," the man said, "and I'm calling the *manager!* Five . . . four . . . three . . . two . . ."

Ed slammed into the counter and fell forward, hugging the register. He stood up straight, balanced himself, then smiled over the counter at the man, saying, "Welcome to Good Burger, home of the Good Burger, can I take your order?"

"Well, it's about *time!*" the man growled, glaring at Ed. "Can I get two Good Burgers . . . *please.*"

"Sorry," Ed said. *"I* have to get 'em. Customers aren't allowed in the back."

The man's mouth bunched up in an ugly little pucker and he slapped a hand onto the counter. "Just give me two Good Burgers!" he shouted.

"Dude, I can't just *give* you two Good Burgers," Ed explained carefully. "You gotta *pay* for 'em!"

"Oh, just . . . just *forget* about it!" the man blustered. "I've had it up to *here* with Good Burger," he grumbled, leveling a hand at his forehead.

Ed immediately stiffened his posture and returned the salute respectfully.

The man shouted, "I can't *wait* till *Mondo Burger* opens!" Then he turned and stormed out. Most of the people standing in line behind him did the same, turning their nose up at Ed as they left.

"Mondo Burger?" Ed asked. He turned around and asked, "What's Mondo Burger?"

Everyone behind the heat lamp trays rolled their eyes. Even Spatch, who was very big, very scary, and usually responded to no one (and who was never, *ever* seen without his spatula), turned and glared at Ed for a long, cold moment. Monique and Fizz approached Ed, looking slightly annoyed.

Pointing out the window, Monique asked, "See that

giant building there across the street? The one they've been building for only *ten months?*"

"Yeah!" Ed exclaimed, amazed. "I see it!"

"That's Mondo Burger," Fizz said.

"They open in, like, three days," Deedee said, wiping her hands on a towel as she came out from the back. "Just another establishment that profits from the slaughter of poor, defenseless cows."

The others looked at her blankly.

Deedee was a staunch vegetarian and worked at Good Burger despite the fact that she opposed the food they served. That's why she only worked on the salads. She refused to touch meat.

"They're opening in three days?" Ed asked. "Well . . . *cool!*"

Mr. Baily appeared as if from nowhere. Mr. Baily *always* appeared as if from nowhere! He was the manager of Good Burger.

"It's *not* cool, Ed," Mr. Baily said with a slight quaver in his voice. "They're competition. *Big* competition."

"They could put us out of business, Ed," Monique said quietly and solemnly.

"Oh, come *on* now," Mr. Baily said with a loud, artificial laugh. "Good Burger has been here for over forty *years!* We're a beloved institution in this town. The people *love* us!" He glanced at Ed. "Well, *most* of us." He looked around at each of them, grinning broadly. But his eyes kept returning to the window. "Don't you worry. No one's going to put *us* out of business." His eyes finally settled on the window . . . on the building across the street. "At least, probably."

10

Fizz, Monique, Deedee, and even Ed turned to look out the window at Mondo Burger.

"Ooohhhh," Mr. Baily groaned miserably as he turned and hurried into the back, toward his office.

"We could be in big trouble," Fizz said.

Ed looked around at the others and muttered, "Uuhhh . . . no?"

Chapter 2

Final exams were in progress at Brierdale High School. And Dexter Reed, one of the students in the process of *taking* a final exam, was sound asleep in his chair. He was leaning back, legs splayed beneath the desktop, head bent forward. Out of it.

"You have *two minutes* to turn in your exams," said Mr. Wheat. He paced the room with hands joined behind his back, glaring at his students with teacherly intimidation. "And there will be *no* exceptions!"

For Dexter, those two minutes passed very quickly . . . because he wasn't even *aware* of them!

The bell rang and Mr. Wheat called, "Time!"

Dexter jerked awake, looked around, then blurted, "Ha-*hah!*" He jumped to his feet and headed for the door along with all the other students.

Mr. Wheat suddenly stepped in front of him and asked, "What's your hurry, Mr. Reed?"

"My hurry is that it's now officially summer vacation," Dexter said with a smile. "And yet, I'm still lookin' at *you*."

"You finished your exam awfully fast," Mr. Wheat said, his eyebrows bunching together at the top of his nose.

"Yeah. Next time you should make it a little more challenging."

Mr. Wheat's lips pulled back over his teeth as his chest puffed up with a deep breath. He released that breath in a long, irritated sigh, glaring down at Dexter through eyes that were narrowed to sliver-like slits. "One of these days, wise guy," he said in a low, breathy voice. *"One* of these *days,* I'm going to—"

"Have a nice summer, Mr. Wheat!" Dexter interrupted. He planted a big kiss on Mr. Wheat's cheek, then rushed out of the room.

Dexter left the school building and headed across the parking lot toward his car.

"Hey, Dexter!"

He turned around to see his friend Jake jogging toward him.

"How do you think you did on your exam?" Jake asked as he and Dexter walked across the parking lot together.

"Sorry, Jake. Summer vacation started, uh . . ." Dexter lifted his arm and checked his wristwatch. ". . . forty-eight seconds ago. That means school, work, or anything of that nature is now officially off limits for the next three months."

1 3

They stopped beside a beautiful Chrysler Sebring convertible.

"Nice car," Jake said. "This yours?"

"Nah, it's my mom's. She's away on a business trip to New York." Dexter opened the driver's side door and got behind the wheel. "C'mon, get in. I'll drive you home."

"She lets you *drive* this when she's out of town?" Jake asked as he got into the car.

Dexter started the car, then put on a pair of sunglasses. "Nope," he said, smiling at Jake. Then he shifted the car into gear and peeled out of the school parking lot.

"Hey, Ed!" Mr. Baily said cheerfully as he approached Ed with a bulging Good Burger bag. "We've got a delivery!"

Ed was standing at the counter, waiting diligently for the next customer.

Mr. Baily said, "Take this Good Meal over to Chief Arlin at the fire station, would ya?"

"But . . . *dude!*" Ed said with wide eyes and a little panic in his voice. "I don't *do* deliveries!"

"You do for the time being. O'Malley was fired."

"He was? How come?"

"He came to work without any pants again. The address is on the bag."

Ed took the bag and smiled. "It shall be delivered!"

Although Dexter had offered to drive Jake home, that's not where they went. They drove all over the place, enjoying the sun in the convertible.

"So, what's your plan for the summer?" Jake asked as they cruised down a street lined with lush, green trees.

"Oh, I figure I'll sleep every day till around noon," Dexter said with a smile. "Then, I'll lay out by the pool, swim a little, Jacuzzi, order out for some Chinese food . . . maybe invite a couple of fine females over to share an egg roll or two. Then, the next day, I'll start over and do it all again."

Jake shook his head. "Jeez, you're lucky. My folks made me get a summer job."

"Well, that's *your* fault," Dexter said. "See, sometimes, you gotta *explain* things to parents. Like . . . summer vacation. The key word is 'va-*cay*-shun.'"

As Dexter and Jake enjoyed the sun in Dexter's mother's convertible, Ed was in the middle of making his first delivery. He skated along, carrying a bagged Good Meal and singing to himself happily: "I'm a dude . . . She's a dude . . . He's a dude . . . 'Cause we're all dudes!"

Ed skated off the sidewalk and started to cross an intersection, but he saw the Sebring coming, and his eyes became almost as wide as his mouth.

"Oooh, *man,*" Ed groaned, just before shouting, at the top of his lungs, *"Whoooaaa!"*

For *just* a moment, Ed and Dexter locked eyes as Ed dove forward to avoid being hit by Dexter's Chrysler.

In the convertible, Dexter and Jake cried, simultaneously, *"Yaaaaaggghhh!"* as Dexter pulled to the right on the steering wheel to avoid Ed.

The Chrysler Sebring slammed into the side of a brand new Ford Probe.

Ed waved as he skated on his way.

For a long moment, Dexter couldn't move. He was too busy staring in *horror* at the front of his mother's car . . . and at the smashed-in side of the Probe!

"Reed! Dexter Reed! Look at this! Look what you've done to my Probe!"

Dexter recognized Mr. Wheat's voice immediately, even though he didn't take his eyes from the mangled connection of the two cars. He *couldn't* take his eyes away.

"Look, don't worry, Jake," Dexter said in a thick whisper. "Just be cool and let me handle this. I'll just—"

Dexter stopped when he heard the sound of running footsteps fading in the distance. He turned to his right and saw that Jake was gone. Looking back over his shoulder at Jake disappearing in the distance, Jake called, "Hey . . . thanks for your *support!*"

Suddenly, Mr. Wheat was glaring down at him.

"Do you know what this car *cost* me?" Mr. Wheat asked.

"Listen, Mr. Wheat, it wasn't my fault! Some crazy *nut* skated right in *front* of me, and—"

"This car cost twenty-two *thousand* dollars!" Mr. Wheat wailed. "And that didn't include the blasted chrome wheels! Or the blasted cassette player!"

Dexter nodded. "Yeah, they always blast you with the blasted extras."

"Shut *up!* Just give me your driver's license!"

Dexter began to squirm. "Uh . . . well, see . . . regarding my driver's license? Uh, see . . . I *will* be gettin' one soon. But, uh . . ."

16

"You're driving without a license? Oh, *great!* That means you don't have any insurance, either!" Mr. Wheat reached into his jacket pocket and pulled out a cell phone. "I'm calling the police!"

"No, no, *wait!*" Dexter cried. "I'll pay for all the damages! Please? If the cops find out I was drivin' without a license, I won't be able to drive until I'm twenty-one! Just . . . please, let me fix your car and make things right. That's all I'm asking. What do you say, Mr. Wheat?"

Still holding his cell phone in his left hand, Mr. Wheat glared down at Dexter for a long moment. Then, he said, "Okay . . . fine."

"All *right!*" Dexter cheered with a grin. He reached out and shook Mr. Wheat's hand enthusiastically. "You're a fine man, Mr. Wheat, a *fine* man! So, uh . . ." Dexter tossed a glance at the mangled side of Mr. Wheat's car. ". . . how much you think it's gonna cost?"

An hour later, Dexter knew *exactly* how much it would cost. He stood in an auto garage with Mr. Wheat as a mechanic approached them with a clipboard. Without uttering a word, the mechanic scribbled on a piece of paper on the clipboard, ripped it off, and handed it to Dexter. After reading it, Dexter shouted, "Nineteen hundred *dollars?* B-buh-but . . . I don't *have* nineteen hundred dollars!"

Mr. Wheat smirked at Dexter with grim satisfaction. "I *see*," he said, removing his cell phone from his jacket pocket again.

"No, no, *wait!*" Dexter shouted. "I-I'll *get* the money! Really! I-I'll . . ." Dexter's throat seemed to close and,

17

for a moment, he couldn't continue, couldn't speak. The words caught in his throat like tiny, sliver-like fishbones.

"You'll *what?*" Mr. Wheat asked, still holding the phone in his hand threateningly.

"I-I'll . . . I'll get a-a-a . . . a suh-suh-summer j-job."

Mr. Wheat's lips peeled back over his teeth in an evil grin as he said, in a thick and oily voice, "Good . . . very good."

Dexter closed his eyes and groaned quietly as he felt his stomach turn inside out with disappointment. His summer vacation, which had begun only minutes ago, had ended just as suddenly.

Chapter 3

Dexter had his summer job later that same day . . . at Mondo Burger.

On the outside, Mondo Burger was a monstrous building awash in bright, garish colors and odd geometric shapes. On the roof stood a gigantic fast food meal, a Mondo Meal monument: a giant burger, a giant shake, and a giant order of French fries. Inside, it was cavernous, with even brighter and uglier colors, and more goofy geometric shapes on the walls. It looked like a plane loaded with crayons had crashed.

With Mondo Burger about to open in a few days, all the new employees—including Dexter—were being put through the last steps of their training. In the restaurant's palatial kitchen, a dozen employees were lined up at a counter. Their trainer was a muscular, thick-necked young man with a buzz cut named Griffen. He wore a silver whistle on a black cord around his neck and paced back and forth along the line of trainees, shouting orders. They were assembling hamburgers in perfectly synchronized steps.

"Bun, patty, toppings, sauce, *assemble!*" Griffen barked as he paced. "Bun, patty, toppings, sauce, *assemble!*"

It was hamburger boot camp! But these were not just *any* hamburgers. They were huge . . . *gigantic!* They were easily *twice* the size of a large hamburger from any other fast food restaurant.

Standing nearby, watching the training exercises intently, were two young men. One of them was Kurt Bozwell, a twenty-year-old with a mouth frozen in a permanent unpleasant smirk. He was good-looking in a hard, mean kind of way. But then, Kurt didn't have to be friendly. He was the manager of Mondo Burger. Standing beside him was one of his best friends, Troy, to whom he'd given a cushy job at Mondo Burger. His other best friend was Griffen, who also worked there.

Griffen walked over to Kurt's side and asked, "So . . . what do you think?"

"Excellent," Kurt said with a nod.

"Echoed," Troy muttered.

Satisfied, Griffen went back to his troops and began shouting orders again. "Bun, patty, toppings, sauce, *assemble!*"

The workers assembled one hamburger after another with stiff, robotic movements, keeping time with the cadence of Griffen's calls. Except for Dexter.

He'd begun having problems early on. He simply

couldn't keep up with Griffen's rapid-fire shouting. Dexter had managed to assemble two burgers completely, but rather sloppily. After that, all he could do was make a mess. Trying hard, he fumbled with the ingredients, clumsily knocking them in all directions as he tried to keep pace. He mumbled to himself as he battled with the buns and patties and lettuce.

"Uh-oh . . . c'mere, you bun . . . whoops, dropped the big beef . . ." He'd abandoned any hope of trying to keep up with Griffen. Now, he was just trying to bring the ingredients together to form something that at least *resembled* a hamburger. He snatched up the beef patty he'd dropped and slapped it onto a bun. "Okay, *get* on there, you . . . hey, where'd my lettuce go?" He turned to the guy next to him, who was busy making one perfect burger after another. "Yo, can I borrow some lettuce?"

The guy ignored him.

Dexter shrugged, then spilled ketchup all over the place.

A shrill whistle blew so suddenly and loudly that Dexter jumped and tossed his half-made hamburger into the air. It slopped to the floor around him and he looked up to see Griffen standing in front of him, scowling.

Kurt's footsteps sounded sharply on the tile floor as he hurried over to the trainees. He pointed at Dexter and snapped, "You!"

"Who?" Dexter asked, looking around.

"*You!* Look at this mess!"

"Well, see," Dexter said, "I was, uh . . . I was tryin' to put the big ol' beef patty on the bottom half of the bun

21

before the tomato gets all slippery with the juiciness . . . and the pickle bits, and uh . . ." He turned to the guy next to him again. "Back me up on this, okay?"

Once again, the guy ignored him and stared straight ahead like all the others.

Kurt grabbed the whistle around Griffen's neck and blew it again.

"Aw, again with the whistle," Dexter said, wincing.

"Shut up!" Kurt shouted. "Just be *quiet!*"

"It'd be a lot *more* quiet if you'd quit blowin' that whistle," Dexter muttered.

"Watch your mouth, you pestiferous little *maggot.*"

"Now . . . I'm familiar with the term 'maggot,' " Dexter said with a frown. "But . . . *pestiferous?*"

Some of the other trainees stifled their laughter.

Kurt leaned close to Dexter. "Burn this into the front row of your brain, Chuckles. If there's one thing Kurt can't stand, it's an incompetent, bumbling, sloppy, fast food employee!"

At the very moment that Kurt was expressing his opinion of incompetent employees, Ed was fixing the malfunctioning milk shake machine over at Good Burger . . . from the *inside!*

The lid atop the machine flipped open and Ed popped out with a wrench in hand. He was covered with a layer of dribbling pink strawberry milk shake.

"Mmmm!" Ed grinned, licking his lips. "My *favorite!*"

Mr. Baily appeared and gasped when he saw Ed.

"Ed!" he cried. "What *are* you doing inside the *milk shake* machine?"

"Tryin' to fix it," Ed said, waving the wrench.

Mr. Baily rolled his eyes and rubbed a hand downward over his face. "Did you turn it *on,* Ed?"

"What?"

"The switch. Did you turn on the *switch?*"

Ed chewed on his lower lip sheepishly as he peered over the edge of the machine and down at the switch on the side. He reached down and flipped it. The machine hummed to life and the mass of strawberry milk shake in which Ed was mostly immersed suddenly began to churn.

"Whooaaa!" Ed blurted, suddenly grinning. "Strawberry Jacuzzi!"

Back at Mondo Burger, all of the employees-in-training had been gathered into a single group. There were dozens of them. They all stood at attention, backs stiff, eyes looking straight ahead . . . except for Dexter, who was kind of fidgety and kept looking all over the place.

Kurt and Griffen stood together now, off to the side, as Troy paced slowly in front of the trainees.

"All right, people, *listen up!*" Troy shouted. "In less than seventy-two hours, Mondo Burger will open. And we're gonna be the biggest thing to hit fast food since . . . since . . . well, since the nugget."

Dexter frowned and muttered to himself, "The *nugget?*"

"Now," Troy went on, "I'm gonna turn it over to

2 3

Mondo Burger's general manager and commander of operations . . . Kurt Bozwell!"

Troy stepped aside as Kurt moved forward to face the politely applauding trainees. Except for Dexter. He didn't applaud.

"Thank you, Troy," Kurt said. He took in a deep breath, then bellowed, *"People!* I am fully *stoked* about being in charge of all of you!" He joined his hands behind his back and lowered his voice, smirking at them. "Once Mondo Burger kicks butt in this town, we'll build more Mondo Burger restaurants. And then more . . . and then *more* after *that!"*

Dexter rolled his eyes and said, under his breath, "We get the picture."

"Within two years, Mondo Burger will be the *biggest* burger chain on the *planet!"* Kurt declared, shooting a stiff forefinger toward the ceiling. "Of course, *first,"* he added with sneering sarcasm, "we've gotta hose our competition across the street . . . Good Burger."

Troy and Griffen chuckled and sneered.

Kurt began to pace before the trainees, saying, "From now on, your *life* is Mondo Burger. That means you gotta bail on all your personal *crap.* Forget your friends, your family. Kurt is now both your mother *and* your father."

Dexter turned to the guy next to him and said, "Jeez, Kurt must look awful strange naked."

Unlike before, the guy began to laugh, then tried to conceal it with a cough.

"Who *said* that?" Kurt shouted. "Who talked while Kurt was talking?"

"It was *him!*" Griffen said, pointing to Dexter. *"He uttered something!"*

Every head in the room turned toward Dexter as Kurt closed in on him, sneering. "I shoulda *known,*" he grumbled as he stopped directly in front of Dexter, their noses almost touching.

"I'm sorry I uttered," Dexter said, his eyes widening.

A few more of the employees tried to conceal their laughter.

"You think you're funny, don't you?" Kurt growled. "Well, there's no room here at Mondo Burger for comedians, bro. You mess with Kurt, you go in the grinder."

"Uh, this *grinder* of yours," Dexter said hesitantly, "is it a *real* grinder . . . or is it some kind of metaphor?"

"That's it, clown!" Kurt shouted. "You're *gone!* Adiosed! TKO'd! Historical! *Toast!"*

"Aw, now wait," Dexter said, raising both hands. "I'm sorry. I won't be funny anymore. I *promise!* See?" Dexter tried to stand at attention and make a serious face. His back remained stiff, but his face just couldn't remain serious.

"Security!" Kurt called.

"Wait!" Dexter said. "C'mon, Kurt . . . *sir* . . . uh, Sir Kurt? Please? I *need* this job!"

Two security guards hurried to Kurt's side and he pointed at Dexter, saying, "Take out the trash!"

Dexter suddenly felt insulted, and a little angry. "Hey, wait just a second!"

"I said," Kurt told the security guards, "get this *loser* outta my *face!"*

"*Loser?*" Dexter shouted. "All right, now you're about to push me a *little* too far!"

The security guards flanked Dexter and grabbed his arms.

Kurt leaned even closer to Dexter and said, "Oh, yeah? You wanna piece of me?"

"Yeah," Dexter growled. "Extra crispy, please." He lunged toward Kurt, but the security guards held him back. Then they began to haul him out of the restaurant. "It's a good thing you called your buddies!" Dexter shouted at Kurt.

Troy and Griffen laughed as they watched Dexter being carried out.

"C'mon, fellas," Dexter said to the security guards, "is this really *necessary?*"

Within seconds, Dexter found himself thrown out onto the sidewalk in front of Mondo Burger. He rolled to a stop on the concrete, then got to his feet quickly and dusted himself off.

A few pedestrians slowed to look at him curiously.

Dexter faced the doorway through which he'd been thrown, shook a fist at Mondo Burger, and shouted, "That's *it!* I *quit!* You're *rude!*" Then he turned and walked away, trying his best to appear casual.

Chapter 4

It was business as usual at Good Burger. Ed was waiting on a customer at the counter.

"Look," the man said, "I ordered *one* Good Burger with *nothing* on it!"

"And that's what I gave you," Ed said innocently.

"No! You gave me a bun . . . *just* a *bun!*" He held the empty bun in front of Ed. "Look, there's no *meat* in here!"

"You said you wanted *nothing* on it," Ed said.

"Yes, but I expected a meat patty!"

"Dude, a meat patty is *something*. You said, *nothing*. Yo, Fizz!" Ed called as Fizz walked by behind him. "Is a meat patty something or nothing?"

"Uh . . . something?" Fizz said, somewhat confused.

Ed smiled at the man. "I win."

"That *rips* it!" the man said, throwing the bun onto the counter. "I'm reporting your name to the manager!"

"The manager already knows my name," Ed said.

The man shuddered with anger. "Oh, I-I-I . . . I'll *see* you in *hell!*"

"Okay, dude, see ya there!" Ed called as the man spun around and hurried toward the exit.

From one of the booths, Dexter watched the man storm out. On the table in front of Dexter were a dozen empty Good Shake cups. Ed walked over to the booth and put another shake on the table.

"Here's another Good Shake," he said.

"Good," Dexter muttered. "Keep 'em coming."

"Don't you think you've had enough?"

"Who are you, my mother?"

Ed checked his name tag curiously, just to make sure.

Dexter's eyes narrowed as he stared up at Ed. He craned his head forward, studying Ed's face. "Hey . . . you look familiar. Don't I know you from somewhere?"

"Maybe," Ed said. "You ever been to Australia?"

"No."

"Me neither."

Dexter continued to stare intently at Ed. "I could *swear* I've seen you someplace before."

Ed's face brightened with a grin. "Hey! Maybe I'm somebody famous, like a baseball player, or a pretty nurse!"

Dexter's face screwed into a confused frown. "What in the *world* are you talking about?"

"Okay, okay, I give up. Who am I?"

Dexter shook his head slowly. "Man, I don't know *who* you are, or *where* I know you from, or *why* you think you're an attractive nurse . . . but I am *sure* that I don't want to know you anymore. Now, go away. I've had a very bad day."

"What's wrong? Were you bitten by a sheep?"

"What?"

"Did you lose your trousers?"

Confused, Dexter glanced down at his pants. *"No!"*

"Sore bladder?"

"Look, you're an unusually bad guesser, so I'll just tell you why I'm upset. I gotta come up with nineteen hundred bucks to fix some jerk's car, another eight hundred to fix my mom's car, and I just got fired."

"So . . . your bladder's fine?"

Dexter rolled his eyes. "Will you *forget* about my *bladder?"*

"I could try," Ed said with a shrug.

"Man, I can't believe *Kurt* fired me from Mondo Burger," Dexter said. He spit the name "Kurt" out with disgust. "He yelled at me, he insulted me, he made fun of me . . ."

"Boy, you must really suck."

Dexter frowned. "See, normally about now, I'd slap you in your head . . . but I'm not sure your brain would understand the concept of pain."

Ed's eyes widened as he grinned again. "Wanna see my belly button?"

Dexter sighed as he stood up to leave, taking his milk shake with him. "Well, it was very unusual to meet you, Ed. I'm gonna go now and try to beg someone for a summer job."

"Why don't you just work here at Good Burger?" Ed asked.

"Here?"

"Hey, Mr. Baily?" Ed called to his boss, who was behind the front counter. "This guy needs a job. Can he have one?"

"No," Mr. Baily said.

"See ya," Dexter said with a wave, heading for the door.

"Wait!" Ed grabbed Dexter's arm, turning to Mr. Baily again. "C'mon, Mr. Baily, he really needs a job! He could do fries."

"Otis does fries."

"Well, yeah, but look at him . . . how much longer could he possibly live?"

Mr. Baily turned and looked at the stooped over, wheezing form of Otis, the oldest living fast food restaurant employee. Thinking about it, Mr. Baily looked Dexter over. "Ever worked in fast food before, uh . . . what's your name?"

Dexter introduced himself, then said, "I have worked in fast food. A little."

"You know how to drive?" Mr. Baily asked.

"Oh, yeah, I'm a *good* driver."

"Any accidents on your record?"

"Not to your knowledge," Dexter replied with a smile.

"All right, kid. I'll give you a chance. You're on deliveries. And you may have to pitch in and do some counter work."

"Cool!" Ed said, grinning. He put an arm around Dexter's shoulders. "I'll teach him everything I know."

Mr. Baily rolled his eyes and muttered, "God help us."

"Don't worry, Mr. Baily," Dexter said. "I won't let you down."

Mr. Baily disappeared into his office as Ed showed Dexter around, introducing him to the others.

"Hey, Fizz! This is Dexter. Dexter, Fizz. Fizz works the drive-through."

"Hi-dee-ho, Dex!" Fizz said enthusiastically.

Dexter smiled. "Hi-dee-ho, Fih!"

Fizz blinked, surprised. "Wow! No one's ever abbreviated *my* name before! I *love* that!"

"This is Otis, Dexter," Ed said. "He's in his eighties, and he still works in fast food."

Otis lifted his head with great effort to look at Dexter. In a weak, quavery voice, he said, "I should've died years ago."

Deedee was brushing her hair over the grill. "And over there is Deedee. She's a veterinarian."

"Vegetarian," Deedee corrected.

"Yeah. That means she won't eat fur."

"I won't *wear* fur," Deedee said. "I don't eat *meat*. No one should. Cows are defenseless creatures."

"If you're against eating meat," Dexter said, "what are you doing working in a burger place?"

"My goal is to start a revolution from within the system," Deedee replied.

Dexter nodded, impressed. "Let me know how it works out."

As they walked farther into the back of the restaurant, Dexter saw Spatch . . . huge and menacing, slightly hunched forward with his spatula clutched in an enormous, meaty fist.

Dexter stopped and clutched Ed's elbow. "Uh, Ed . . . what is *that?*"

"Oh, that's Spatch. He's our cook."

Spatch turned his enormous head to look their way and made a guttural growl. A fly buzzed around his head frantically.

Lowering his voice, Ed leaned close to Dexter and said, "Spatch isn't exactly, um . . . a *people* person."

The fly landed on Spatch's nose. For a moment, Spatch's eyes crossed, then he swatted himself *hard* in the face with the spatula, killing the fly.

"Hey!" Monique said to Spatch, looking disgusted. "You wanna rinse that off before you use it again?"

Dexter's eyes widened when he saw Monique . . . and his heart skipped a beat. He stepped toward her, flashed his biggest smile, and said, "Well, hellooooo. I'm Dexter, your new coworker."

"I'm Monique."

Dexter reached out, took her hand and shook it. But he didn't let go.

"That's a very handsome paper hat you're wearing. And those green stripes on your uniform really bring out the color of your eyes."

"Yes," Monique said, smiling. "You can imagine how embarrassed I was when I came to work and saw everyone else wearing the same outfit."

Surprising himself, Dexter let out a hearty, genuine laugh as he released her hand. Not only was she beautiful . . . she had a sense of *humor!* "Uh, I guess I'll see you later."

"I guess you will," Monique said, going back to work.

As he walked away with Ed, Dexter said, "Ooohh, she is all *that!*"

"All what?" Ed asked.

"Forget it. Hey . . . so what do I make my deliveries in? A truck? A van?"

"I'll show you," Ed said.

They went to the garage behind the Good Burger building, and Ed opened the door to reveal . . . the Burgermobile! It was a light blue car with the front molded into a giant Good Burger and tires dressed up to look like huge pickle slices.

"This," Ed said reverently, "is the Burgermobile. Think you can handle her?"

"I don't know," Dexter said hesitantly. "I've never driven a sandwich before."

Ed opened the driver's side door and said, "Hop in! I'll take you for a spin!" Dexter got into the Burgermobile reluctantly as Ed started the engine.

"You can drive, right?" Dexter asked nervously. "I mean, you can read all those street signs and—"

Ed peeled out of the garage and shot into the street, turning sharply. The Burgermobile sped down the street, tires squealing with every turn. Dexter fumbled with the seat belt until it was fastened snugly around him, then he clutched the edges of the seat for dear life.

"Whooaaa!" Ed cried. "Now *this* is fast food!"

"Yeah, yeah," Dexter said. "Just look out for the—"

Ed drove the Burgermobile straight through a red light. Other cars honked their horns as they squealed to a halt.

"That was a *red light!*" Dexter shouted.

Ed glanced at him and said, "Uuhhh . . . no?"

With his attention diverted, Ed took the next turn a little too wide . . . a *lot* too wide. The Burgermobile was headed straight for a mailbox at the edge of a sidewalk in front of a house . . .

. . . and at that very moment, the occupant of that house was on his way to the mailbox to get his mail. And it was Mr. Wheat.

"Oh, *nooo!*" Dexter cried.

The Burgermobile jumped the curb and flattened the mailbox like a twig, then turned back onto the road and drove on . . . as Mr. Wheat stood in front of his house, glaring angrily.

"Thank you, Ed!" Dexter snapped.

"You're welcome," Ed said with a grin.

"Thank you for making my life even *worse!*" Dexter said as the Burgermobile raced on down the street.

Chapter 5

Dexter settled into his job quickly. He got along with everyone at Good Burger and even managed to enjoy his job.

On his third night at Good Burger, Dexter stood behind the counter as Otis swept up. His dinner, a wrapped Good Burger, was on the counter in front of him. He frowned thoughtfully as he muttered to himself, "Let's see . . . five dollars an hour, six hours a day, five days a week . . . that means I'll be able to pay for the car in . . ." He counted on his fingers. ". . . another lifetime," he said, his shoulders sagging.

Dexter jumped when the front doors were kicked open suddenly. Kurt Bozwell walked in, followed closely by Troy and Griffen. Kurt strutted in and looked around with his constant smirk, shaking his head slowly.

"Man," Kurt said, approaching the counter, "this

place is the most nauseating, pathetic *hole* I've ever seen. What kind of diseased *maggot* would *eat* here?"

Ed stepped up to the counter and smiled enthusiastically, saying, "Welcome to Good Burger, home of the Good Burger, can I take your order?"

Dexter went to Ed's side immediately, knowing Ed wasn't dealing with just *any* customers.

"Hey, check it, boys!" Kurt called to his friends as he pointed at Dexter. "It's the *reject!*"

Troy and Griffen laughed sneeringly.

"Hey, check it, Ed," Dexter said with a grin. "It's the Mondo idiot!"

With a friendly nod, Ed said, "Oh, nice to meet you, Mondo idiot! I'm Ed."

Kurt leaned over the counter and pushed his face close to Ed's. "Yeah? Well, Ed . . . you just better watch your *butt.*"

"Okay," Ed said. He craned his head around to look at his butt, but found he couldn't crane his head around quite enough. He began to stumble around in a circle, trying to look at his butt, like a dog chasing his tail.

"You got some reason to be here, Kurt?" Dexter asked.

"Yeah," Kurt said. "I just thought you Good Burger losers should be aware that *tonight* is the grand opening of Mondo Burger. And the second we open our doors . . . Good Burger goes in the grinder."

"Again with the grinder," Dexter said. "Look, either order something, or get out."

"Sure," Kurt sneered. "You can take my order. I'll have

36

the *last* Good Burger." He snatched up Dexter's burger from the counter. "To *go.*" He tore the wrapper open and took a big bite from the burger, then laughed with his mouth full . . . and open. He turned and left Good Burger, with Troy and Griffen behind him, laughing.

Ed finally stopped spinning around. He swayed back and forth as he stared at Dexter with wide, wobbly eyes. "I give up! There is no *way* a guy can watch his own *butt!*"

Later that night, the entire Good Burger gang was staring out the window at the Mondo Burger festivities across the street. Two rotating spotlights shot bars of white light into the night sky and sparkling lights of every color blinked and flashed around the restaurant as a huge crowd gathered. A small spotlight focused on an elevated stage where a metal box was set on a three-foot-tall stand beside a microphone.

Kurt Bozwell stepped up to the microphone and asked loudly, "Is everyone lovin' my party?" His question was met with raucous cheers and loud applause. "Today kicks off a radical new frontier in fast food," Kurt said. "Big burgers, but *not* at big prices!" There was more applause. "And now . . . I am psyched to present to you . . . *Mondo Burger!*" He turned, grabbed the lever beside the box and jerked it hard.

Against the black night sky, a mammoth hamburger, bag of fries, and milk shake suddenly lit up like giant mythic gods.

All the lights inside Good Burger buzzed and flickered

as Ed and Dexter and all the others tilted their heads back to look at the dimming lights. They finally blinked out, leaving everyone in darkness.

Across the street, Kurt left the elevated stage, and the crowd followed him to the front entrance to Mondo Burger . . . two enormous glass doors that stood tall, like the gates to a castle. A fat red ribbon stood between the crowd and the doors.

Smirking, Kurt held up a large pair of scissors and said, "And now, people . . . *welcome to Mondo Burger!*" He cut the ribbon, then stepped aside as the crowd poured into the enormous, brightly lit restaurant, in which a band played music and the delicious smell of gigantic burgers filled the air.

The Good Burger gang sat in darkness, watching the glamorous grand opening of Mondo Burger through the window.

"Uh, Mr. Baily," Dexter said. "Seein' as we got no customers or electricity, uh . . ."

"All right," Mr. Baily said with a sigh. "Maybe we should all just go on home." After a moment, Mr. Baily blurted, *"Hey!* What's that in my pocket?"

"Oh, sorry," Ed said. "I thought that was *my* pocket!"

"Jeepers, Ed!" Mr. Baily barked. "It's not *that* dark, *is* it?"

"Well, kinda," Ed said with an embarrassed chuckle.

"Okay, everyone," Mr. Baily said. "See you tomorrow."

The grand opening festivities at Mondo Burger were grand. The lines at the counter for the giant Mondo

Burgers were long, and the music was loud. People waiting in line danced with one another, and the cavernous restaurant echoed with the sound of gleeful laughter. Everyone was having a *great* time.

Kurt, Troy, and Griffen stood at the front of the restaurant, looking out the window at the darkened Good Burger restaurant across the street.

"Looks like Good Burger closed early tonight," Troy said.

"Yep," Kurt said with a cold chuckle. "And pretty soon . . . they'll be closed for *good.*"

Chapter 6

During the next week, Mondo Burger did mondo business . . . while Good Burger's business went rapidly, steadily downhill.

As customers formed long lines outside Mondo Burger, waiting to get in, the employees at Good Burger sat around the empty restaurant with nothing to do but blow straw wrappers at each other.

While Mondo Burger employees piled their gigantic hamburgers on tables for eager, hungry customers . . . Ed stacked a few dozen wrapped, unpurchased Good Burgers into a pyramid, until it collapsed and the burgers scattered in all directions around him.

Mondo Burger employees stacked their overflowing cash drawers on Kurt's desk as Kurt grinned greedily at all the money . . . while Dexter snoozed snoringly in the Burgermobile.

Late one day, with only one customer in Good

Burger—a little old lady who sat in a corner booth trying to keep her teeth in while she ate—Mr. Baily hurried into the restaurant.

"Got one!" he called, holding up a paper bag as he went behind the counter.

"Got one what?" Monique asked.

"A Mondo Burger."

"Ooohh!" Fizz said, hurrying over to Mr. Baily with his usual enthusiasm. "Let's see it!"

"All right," Mr. Baily said, pulling the enormous burger from the bag and putting it on the counter. "Don't get all excited, now." He unwrapped the burger as his employees gathered around him to get a good look at what the competition had to offer.

"It's *huge*," Monique said.

Spatch scooped his spatula under the hamburger and lifted it from the counter. The Mondo Burger was so big and so heavy that the spatula bent weakly under its weight. Spatch's upper lip curled back over his teeth and he growled at the burger, dropping it back onto the counter. He turned and went back to the kitchen.

"And they charge the same as we do for a Good Burger," Mr. Baily said, frowning as he shook his head. "This is not good."

While Fizz went to the register to count money, Ed picked up the Mondo Burger and gazed at it in amazement. "Whooaaa!" he blurted. "How do they *do* it?"

Dexter shrugged and said, "They just use more meat."

"Poor cows," Deedee said, clicking her tongue sadly.

"Spatch, toss me a Good Burger!" Ed called over his shoulder.

41

A Good Burger sailed from the back and Ed plucked it out of the air. He held it to his ear while holding the Mondo Burger to his other ear. Then he wobbled them back and forth a little.

"Hmmm," he said. "They *sound* similar."

Mr. Baily walked over to Fizz at the register and asked, "So . . . what was our take today?"

"Forty-three dollars and nine cents."

"Oh, well," Mr. Baily said with a sigh, scrubbing a hand downward over his long, sad face. "I guess I can always feed my mother *cat* food."

"So," Dexter said, "this is probably not the best time to ask for a raise?"

Mr. Baily shot Dexter a hard look. "Not *exactly,* no," he said. "I'm going home. Mind locking up, Ed?"

Ed suddenly stiffened and grabbed his head with both his hands, lips pulled back over clenched teeth. "Uh . . . yeah. Makes it hard to think!"

Mr. Baily rolled his eyes and sighed. "Monique? Lock up, will ya?"

"It's handled," she said.

"G'night, people."

Mr. Baily shuffled out of the restaurant, shoulders sagging and head hanging low.

"So, Monique," Dexter said, smiling, "what are you gonna do tonight, uh, after you lock up?"

"I thought I'd go home," she replied.

Ed started putting on his Rollerblades.

"Home?" Dexter asked. "How come?"

"Well, that's where all my stuff is," she said casually.

She headed for the kitchen, paying no attention to Dexter.

Dexter stared at the spot where Monique had been standing, then smiled. "Hah! I get it! Home . . . stuff . . . that was *good!*" He turned to follow Monique, saying, "You know, you're really very funny with the—"

"Hey, Dexter!" Ed said, standing up on his Rollerblades. "Whatta you say *we* hang out tonight?"

Ed skated toward Dexter clumsily, arms flailing.

"Hey!" Dexter shouted, eyes widening as Ed shot toward him. "Careful, Ed!"

"Whooaaa!" Ed shouted as he lost control of his skates. He sped by Dexter, barely missing him. But for a split second, Ed and Dexter locked eyes . . . just as they had when Ed had skated in front of Dexter's car.

Ed rolled on, and slammed into poor old Otis, who wasn't expecting a collision of *any* kind. Otis was knocked to the floor, but Ed rolled on until he hit a wall.

Fizz rushed to Otis's side and helped him up.

"Am I dead yet?" Otis asked. "Did that kill me?"

"No, Otis," Fizz said, "you're fine."

"Oh," Otis said with a frown. "Darn."

But Dexter was paying no attention to Otis. His eyes were slowly widening as he suddenly realized where he'd seen Ed before. He spun around and faced Ed, who was pushing himself away from the wall.

"Wait a minute!" Dexter exclaimed. *"You!"* He pointed a finger at Ed and began to step toward him.

"Me?" Ed asked, pointing a finger at his own chest.

"Now I know where I saw you before!" Dexter said, his voice raising as he approached Ed. *"You're* the in-line

43

skatin' *nut!"* He poked Ed's chest with his forefinger. *"You* caused my car wreck!"

Ed's smile dropped away and his eyes became huge as he said, "Uuhhh . . . no?"

"You did *too* cause my wreck!" Dexter shouted. "You're the reason I owe nineteen hundred *bucks!* You're the reason my mom found out I was driving without a license! You cost me a *fortune!* You ruined my *summer!* You wrecked my *life!"*

Ed stared at Dexter for a moment, his mouth hanging open. Then he asked, "So, uh . . . you *don't* wanna hang out tonight?"

"No!" Dexter barked. "I don't wanna hang out with you . . . *ever!"*

Dexter spun around and stormed away from Ed, heading for the door . . . but he stumbled to a stop when Otis hobbled in front of him.

"Do you think you could help me get to a hospital?" Otis asked, clutching his side. "I think I've broken a bone."

"Aw . . . sure, come on," Dexter said. He put an arm around Otis, shot an angry look at Ed, then helped Otis out of the restaurant.

The next day, Good Burger was even emptier than the day before. Across the street, crowds of people poured into Mondo Burger, eager to bury their teeth into the huge burgers Mondo Burger sold for the *same* price as the *much* smaller Good Burgers.

Mr. Baily paced back and forth in front of the counter while Dexter ate his lunch in a booth.

Ed stood behind the counter. Before him were a Good

44

Burger and a Mondo Burger. He examined them both with a magnifying glass.

Mr. Baily stopped pacing and spun around to face Ed behind the counter.

"Ed!" Mr. Baily barked. "Put that Mondo Burger *away!*"

"But how do they *do* it?" Ed asked. "It's huge! *Huge,* I tell ya!"

"They obviously use more *beef!*" Mr. Baily snapped. "Just get back to work. I'm gonna get back to work and . . . be sad."

Mr. Baily went behind the counter and disappeared into his office.

A customer walked in through the door. But not just *any* customer. It was Mr. Wheat. He stepped over to the booth in which Dexter was sitting, eating his lunch.

"Ah," Mr. Wheat said with a cold grin, "Mr. Reed. Hard at work as usual, I *see.*" Holding his Good Burger between both hands, Dexter looked up at Mr. Wheat cautiously.

"I am havin' my *lunch,*" Dexter said.

"I just stopped by to tell you," Mr. Wheat said, "I picked up my car from the body shop. Good as new." He handed Dexter a slip of paper. "Here's the receipt."

Dexter dropped his burger on a napkin as he gawked at the receipt, mouth open and eyes wide.

"Twenty-five hundred *dollars?*" Dexter cried. "The estimate was only *nineteen* hundred!"

"That's why they call it an *estimate,*" Mr. Wheat said.

Dexter slumped back in the booth and gawked at the receipt.

"Now," Mr. Wheat went on, *"I* estimate that you have approximately two and a half months left to come up with my money."

Dexter looked up to see Mr. Wheat grinning down at him icily.

"Good day, Mr. Reed," Mr. Wheat said flatly. "I'm off to have my lunch . . . at Mondo Burger."

Mr. Wheat spent another moment or two glaring and grinning down at Dexter, then turned and left Good Burger.

Dexter stared at the receipt for a long time, then lowered his head and groaned, "Twenty . . . five . . . *hundred!* Oohhh . . . it *hurts!"*

Ed approached Dexter's booth carrying a tray of food: a Good Burger, a large bag of fries, and a Good Shake. He slid into the booth across from Dexter and put the tray on the table.

"Hey, Dex," Ed said, smiling, "mind if I sit here?"

Dexter leaned back, annoyed, and said, "Yes, I *do* mind!"

Ed settled into the booth anyway.

"Uh . . . what are you *doin'?"* Dexter asked.

"Havin' lunch," Ed said.

"I *told* you not to *sit* here!" Dexter cried. "I don't *like* you!"

Smiling, Ed removed a long French fry from the bag on his tray.

Dexter said, "Can you get that through your head?"

Ed stared at the French fry.

"I can *try,"* he said.

Ed tried to shove the long French fry into his right ear. The French fry bent. Ed turned it around and tried to shove the *other* end into his ear. Once again, the French fry bent.

"Nope," Ed said. "I can't get it through my head."

Dexter rolled his eyes.

"All right," Dexter said. "I guess I'm gonna have to spell this out for ya. I don't wanna have lunch with you, I don't wanna sit by you, and I don't wanna see you."

As Dexter spoke, Ed produced a bunch of grapes he'd found in the kitchen and plopped it onto the table. He plucked off two grapes and stuck one in each of his nostrils, then stared directly at Dexter.

"I don't wanna smell you," Dexter continued, "I don't wanna hang out with you . . . I don't even wanna use words with the letter 'U'"!

Ed grinned, and when he spoke, his voice was very pinched and nasal, because of the grapes in his nose.

"Look at me!" Ed said cheerfully. "I'm grape nose boy!" He waved his arms around wildly and babbled, "Bloobidy, bloobidy, bloobidy!"

"Stop that!" Dexter shouted, suddenly annoyed by Ed's nonsense. "C'mon . . . quit it! Take the grapes outta your nose!"

Ed continued to wave his arms around wildly and babble, "Bloobidy, bloobidy, bloobidy!"

Suddenly, in spite of his own annoyance, Dexter laughed.

"C'mon," Dexter said, trying to swallow his laughter, "take the grapes . . ."

But he found himself laughing even harder. He leaned back and guffawed as he watched Ed waggle his head back and forth with grapes in his nostrils.

"It's not funny!" Dexter said as he continued to laugh.

"Hah!" Ed said. "Made you laugh!"

"So?" Dexter said, holding his stomach as he tried to calm his own laughter. "Oh, I give *up!*"

Smiling, Ed pulled the grapes from his nostrils. He offered one to Dexter.

"Grape?" Ed asked politely.

Dexter pulled away and grimaced. "Uh . . . I'll pass."

Ed ate both of the grapes, grinning as he chewed them.

Dexter stared in shock, his mouth hanging open.

"Problem?" Ed asked as he chewed.

"Uh . . . well, I shoulda figured lunch with you would be . . . uh, different," Dexter said.

"Well," Ed said, "I've still got a Good Burger to eat, don't I?" He smiled as he pulled a small container from his pocket. He removed the top bun from the burger, turned the container upside down over the patty and began to pound on it. A bit of orange goo spattered from the container and onto the burger patty.

"What's that *goo?*" Dexter asked.

"My sauce," Ed said, as he continued to pound on the container. "I make it myself."

"You carry your own *sauce?*"

The sauce suddenly came out in a gush and some of it splashed on Dexter.

"Aw, would you be *careful?*" Dexter barked, grabbing a napkin and wiping the goo from his shirt.

"Sorry!" Ed said, still trying to get the goo out of the container and onto his burger patty.

Dexter got some of the sauce on his finger and licked it off. His eyes opened wide as he smacked his lips. He reached over, grabbed one of Ed's French fries and dipped it into the glob of sauce on Ed's Good Burger patty, then stuffed it into his mouth.

"Mmmm!" Dexter mmmed, licking his lips. "This sauce is *good!* You *sure* you made this by yourself?"

"Yeah," Ed replied. "It's my own recipe." Ed replaced the top bun and put the container of sauce back in his pocket.

Dexter asked, "Does anyone *else* know about this?"

"No," Ed said.

Dexter leaned back in his seat for a moment. His creative juices were flowing . . . the wheels of his mind were spinning. And when everything finally came together, his face was lit up by a wide grin.

"Hey, Fih!" Dexter called. "C'mere!"

Fizz hurried over to the booth. "Hiya! What can I—"

Dexter grabbed Ed's burger and shoved it into Fizz's mouth, shutting him up.

Fizz frowned, bit down on the burger, then pulled it out of his mouth. He chewed for a moment, then asked, "Hey, why'd you . . . *mmm!*" he said, his eyebrows popping up high. "That's *good!* What'd you put on this?"

Grinning, Dexter called, "Hey, Deedee, Otis, Monique! Get over here!"

As everyone was trying Ed's sauce, Mr. Baily was in his office, on the phone.

"You *know* I think you're pretty," he said. "You're *gorgeous!* Yes, yes . . . I *love* you!"

He heard a sudden murmur of raised voices in the front of the restaurant and frowned.

"Mom, I'll have to call you back, okay? Okay? Please . . . well, yes, you're *still* pretty . . . but I'll have to call you back. So long!"

He hung up the phone and tilted his head, listening. The raised voices continued. He *knew* that something *had* to be wrong. He stood, left his office, and went out into the front of the restaurant.

When Mr. Baily saw all of his employees gathered around one booth, he muttered, "What in the name of ground beef . . . ?"

Dexter spotted him and waved him over, grinning. "Mr. Baily! C'mere and try this!"

As Mr. Baily approached the booth, Dexter dipped a French fry into Ed's sauce, then shoved it into his boss's mouth.

Mr. Baily started to protest . . . but then he began to chew. His lips smacked loudly, and his *eyes* grew wider and wider. His mouth spread into a grin as he said, "This is . . . *marvelous!* What *is* this?"

Ed stood, looking concerned. "Mr. Baily?" he said, speaking very slowly, as if his boss were incredibly stupid. "It's . . . a . . . French . . . fry!"

"No, *no!*" Mr. Baily grumbled. "The *sauce!* Where did this sauce *come* from?"

"Ed made it himself!" Dexter said happily.

"This is *excellent!*" Monique exclaimed.

"It's *awesome!*" Deedee declared.

Smacking his lips, Otis looked at Mr. Baily with a half smile and said, "It makes me glad I'm not dead."

Dexter pulled Ed from the booth and asked, "Do you realize what'll happen if we start puttin' this stuff on Good Burgers?"

Ed stared at him for a moment, then replied, "They'll get all covered with sauce?"

"No!" Dexter replied. "Well, yeah, but . . . just *listen*, okay? If we put that sauce on Good Burgers, everyone'll wanna *eat* here! We'll knock Mondo Burger off the *map!*"

"Ed!" Mr. Baily shouted suddenly. "Get in that kitchen and start makin' *sauce!*"

Ed looked at Mr. Baily, at all his fellow Good Burger employees, then at Dexter, his new friend . . . then he said, with a grin, "It shall be done!"

Chapter 7

When Good Burger opened the next day, the building was adorned with signs and banners with big, bold letters and a lot of exclamations. The signs proclaimed the arrival of Good Burger's delicious new Ed's Sauce.

Inside, a huge banner was strung from one wall to the other above the front counter. The banner read: TRY OUR ALL-NEW ED'S SAUCE!!!

Good Burger quickly filled with curious, hungry customers eager to see what all the fuss was about. When they started eating their hamburgers, the restaurant rang with the exclamations of happy customers:

"Excellent!"

"*Great* sauce!"

"Awesome! Wow!"

"More sauce! It's *fantastic!*"

Mr. Baily approached Ed behind the counter, grinning. He took Ed aside, saying, "Ed! Ed! *Look* at all these *customers!* Good Burger's back in the game! *Hah!* Move over, Mondo Burger!"

"Move over!" Ed agreed happily.

"And as long as you keep making your sauce for us," Mr. Baily assured him, "Good Burger's gonna give you ten cents for every burger we sell!"

At the register, Deedee was overwhelmed by all the customers.

"I'll go help Deedee," Mr. Baily said. "You make more sauce!" He threw his arms around Ed and hugged him hard, then pushed him toward the kitchen.

As Ed began to make more sauce in the kitchen, Dexter sauntered in.

"Hey, Ed!" he said. "How's the sauce comin'?"

"Cool!" Ed replied. "Mr. Baily says it's gonna save Good Burger."

"Yeah, yeah. Now, Ed . . . you remember, it was *my* idea to put your sauce on Good Burgers . . . *right?*"

"Sure. Hey, you know . . . *you* should get some of the money I'm making!"

"I'm glad to hear you say that," Dexter said with a greedy grin. "In fact, since we're gonna be in business together, I thought we should sign a contract. You know, to make our partnership official." Dexter removed a contract and a pen from his jacket pocket and handed them to Ed.

"Hey!" Ed exclaimed as he looked over the contract. "I know some of these words! What does this all mean?"

"It's simple. See, of all the money that Good Burger

gives you for that sauce, you get to keep *twenty percent!* Cool, huh? Okay, see, and then, *I* keep the other *eighty* percent. So, it all works out cool for both of us."

Ed stared into space a moment, almost looking as if he were thinking. "Okay!"

As Ed signed the contract, Dexter said, *"Yes! All right!"* When Ed was finished, Dexter took the contract and looked at it. "Aw, you spelled *Ed* wrong!"

"Sorry," Ed said, taking the contract back. Ed fixed his signature, then handed the contract back to Dexter, who folded it up and put it back in his pocket.

Deedee burst into the kitchen with wide eyes, saying, "Ed! There must be *fifty* customers out there! It's unbelievable! What do you put *in* that sauce?"

"Well," Ed said, "you start off with some ketchup, add a little lemon juice, and—"

Dexter dove forward and tackled Ed, pinning him to the kitchen floor.

"Listen to me carefully!" Dexter barked. "Do *not* tell *anyone* the recipe for that sauce!"

"Oh," Ed said, "you start off with some ketchup, add a little lemon juice and—"

"Stop it! Stop *talking!"* Dexter shouted. "Listen even *more* carefully! Never . . . *ever* tell *anyone* the ingredients of your sauce! You gotta keep it a *secret!* You wanna save Good Burger, don't you?"

"Sure! Good Burger's my *life!"*

"Then you've *got* to keep your sauce recipe a secret! All right?"

54

"Okay."

They were both silent for a moment, then Ed said, "Uh, Dexter? You're squishin' my pancreas."

Across the street, Kurt Bozwell stood in his office with Troy and Griffen. He was looking out his window with a pair of binoculars, staring directly through the window of Good Burger at the busy register.

"It's unbelievable," Kurt growled. "Two days ago, we had Good Burger *crushed*. And *now* look at 'em."

"It's the sauce, boss," Troy said.

Kurt dropped the binoculars and let them hang from around his neck. He turned and smacked Troy in the forehead, saying, *"Duh. I know that. Do I look stupid?"* Kurt turned to Griffen. "I want Good Burger out of business. Find out what's in that sauce."

"I'll get some and have it checked out," Griffen said. He turned and hurried out of the office.

Kurt went back to the window, lifted the binoculars to his eyes and glared at the long line of customers at the counter in Good Burger. As he watched Ed and Dexter laughing and smiling as they waited on customers, Kurt ground his teeth together, making an ugly crunching sound.

After closing time, Mr. Baily wore a look of blissful delight as he counted the money in the cash drawer.

"Ed, here's your take for the day," Mr. Baily said, handing Ed some cash. "Sixty-seven dollars! Thanks for the sauce, kid."

As Mr. Baily trotted back to his office, Ed stared in wonder at the money in his hand, saying, "Whooaaa!"

Dexter walked up and plucked the cash from Ed's hand and began shuffling through it.

"Here, Ed," Dexter said, separating the money. "You get to keep, uh . . . thirteen dollars."

"Wow!" Ed exclaimed as Dexter handed him his share of the money. "That's almost *fourteen dollars!"*

"Uh . . . yeah. Well, see you tomorrow." Dexter turned and headed for the door, counting his money.

Ed called, "Hey, Dex! Where're you goin'? You wanna hang out, or somethin'?"

Dexter stopped and turned to Ed, pocketing the money. "Gee . . . I dunno." When he saw Ed's wide-eyed, hopeful expression, Dexter felt a little guilty. "Well . . . sure. Let's hang out."

Ed grinned, pleased. "Cool! Wanna see my secret place?"

"Uh . . . that's not what I had in mind."

"C'mon!"

Ed led Dexter out of the restaurant and around to a brick wall at the back of the building. There was a ladder leaning against the wall leading up to the roof.

"Follow me," Ed said as he went to the brick wall. Standing right next to the ladder, Ed reached up and clutched the bricks, dug the toe of his shoe between a couple of them, and began to struggle up the wall with difficulty. He managed to get a few inches up the side of the building, grunting and gasping for breath with every inch.

"Welcome to Good Burger, home of the Good Burger, can I take your order?"

"You are in serious trouble!"

"Whoa! Strawberry Jacuzzi!"

"I've never driven a sandwich before."

"You mess with Kurt, you go in the grinder."

"This is where I come to think . . . I think."

"How do they do it? It's huge! Huge, I tell ya!"

"We'll knock Mondo Burger off the map!"

"Since he's chestnut colored, I named him . . . Blueberry."

"We're just looking for the ladies' rest room."

"Whoooaa! Cool place!"

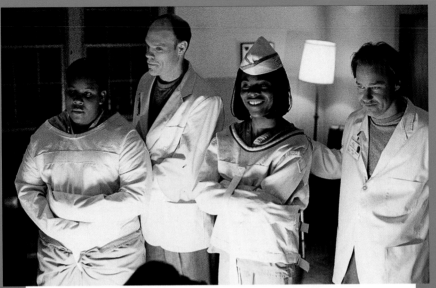

"Here's your 'delivery' from Good Burger."

"I bet you guys got some moves. Feel the rhythm."

"Uh, Mister Scary Man? Can you help us open one of these windows?"

"Adios, Mondo Burger!"

Frowning, Dexter said, "Hey, Ed . . . why don't you use the ladder?"

Ed looked at the ladder beside him for a moment, then dropped to the ground and started up the ladder. He smiled down at Dexter and said, "This is *much* easier!"

As Dexter followed Ed up the ladder, he asked, "Where are you going?"

"To my secret place."

Climbing onto the roof, Dexter looked around. It was surprisingly cozy, with a couple of old chairs and a beautiful view of the stars.

"This is my place," Ed said proudly. "This is where I come to . . . think. I *think."*

"Huh. I didn't take you for much of a thinker."

"Oh, yeah," Ed said as they both seated themselves in the chairs. "I think about Good Burger . . . squirrels . . . cardboard boxes . . . types of cheeses . . . things that are sticky . . ."

Dexter chuckled. "I bet you don't have *one* real problem."

"I got six toes on my left foot. What problems do you have?"

"Other than the ones *you* caused me?" Dexter asked, giving Ed a sidelong glance. "A lot. Most of 'em started when I was a little kid." He leaned back in the chair and looked up at the night sky. "That's when my dad left me and my mom. We must've lived in fifteen places since then."

"Yeah, I kinda have the same situation," Ed said. "My

parents have always been together. They're always telling me how much they love me. And we've lived in the same house ever since I was born."

Dexter gave him a weird look and said sarcastically, "I see what you mean. The similarities are uncanny."

"Not canny at all."

Dexter sighed, looking up at the stars again. "I remember the last time I saw my dad. I was seven years old. And, for no real reason, he brought me this yo-yo. It was so cool. I mean, it wasn't just a regular yo-yo. It had these lights that lit up when you yo-yo'd it. Red lights on one side, blue lights on the other. And it made this funky whistlin' noise, too."

"Sounds like quite a yo-yo. You still got it?"

"Nah. After a while, it stopped lightin' up. Then it quit makin' the whistlin' sound. And then . . . I think my mom just threw it away. You know . . . I don't even remember what my dad looks like."

"I don't remember what *my* dad looks like, either," Ed said. "But at least I get to see him every day."

"Aw, I give up," Dexter said, standing. "I'm goin' home."

Ed followed him to the edge of the roof where Dexter started back down the ladder.

"Hey, Dex . . . thanks for hangin' with me. Y'know."

"Whatever. See ya tomorrow, buddy."

Ed's face lit up as Dexter disappeared down the ladder. He leaned over the edge of the roof and called, "Ya *mean* it?"

On the ground, Dexter looked up at him. "Mean what?"

"That I'm your buddy? You called me your *buddy!*"
Ed was grinning.

"Uh . . . sure. I guess. See ya." Dexter waved, then disappeared around the corner of the building.

Ed went back to his chair and stared up at the stars, still grinning happily.

Chapter 8

The next day, Good Burger was mobbed once again by hungry customers. But the Good Burger gang worked as smoothly as a well-oiled machine. Monique took orders, Fizz filled drinks, Otis fried the French fries, Dexter worked the cash register, and Ed manned the drive-through window.

A big black Chevy Yukon with smoked windows pulled up to the drive-through. The driver's-side window slid down with an electric hum and Kurt Bozwell smirked unpleasantly, wearing a pair of reflective Ray-Bans.

Ed smiled and said, "Welcome to Good Burger, home of the Good Burger, can I take your order?"

"Yeah. Gimme a Good Burger. With extra, extra, *extra* sauce."

"Sorry, dude," Ed said. "Only one glop of sauce per Good Burger. We're runnin' low. It's *way* popular, ya know."

"Well, if you can't give me extra sauce," Kurt said, removing his Ray-Bans, "then tell me . . . how do you make it?"

"Easy! You start with a little ketchup, add some lemon juice, a pinch of—"

A hand reached around and slapped over Ed's mouth from behind. Dexter leaned forward and glared out the window at Kurt. "What're *you* doin' here?" Dexter asked.

"None of your business, loser."

"I know what you're up to." Dexter's eyes narrowed. "Well, *forget* it! We'll never tell you the recipe for that sauce. Right, Ed?" He removed his hand from Ed's mouth.

"—paprika, and some—" Ed continued, without missing a beat.

Dexter clapped his hand over Ed's mouth again and said to Kurt, "Just get outta here."

Kurt gave Dexter an ugly grin. "And what if Kurt don't *feel* like it?"

Dexter held up a mop that had been leaning against the wall just inside the window. "Then Kurt gets his tonsils cleaned with this mop."

Kurt's grin fell away. "Dude, I don't take that kinda crap."

"What kinda crap *do* you take?" Dexter snapped.

"That tears it!" Kurt leaned out of the Yukon and grabbed Ed with one hand and Dexter with the other, trying to pull them out of the drive-through window.

Monique spotted the problem and reacted quickly.

61

"Hey, Spatch!" she called. "There's a guy out here who just called you a big wuss!"

A moment later, Spatch pulled Ed and Dexter from Kurt's grip and leaned out the window, wielding his spatula and growling like an animal.

"Uh, well, Kurt's gotta jam!" Kurt said, dropping back into the Yukon and replacing his sunglasses. He revved the engine, saying, "Hey, maybe I'll give you all new jobs after I put this pus dump outta business!" Then he sped away, tires screeching.

"You ain't puttin' *nobody* outta business!" Dexter called after him.

Spatch agreed with a grunt.

"That guy gives me a rash," Monique said.

"Well, don't worry," Dexter said. "I won't let him bother you."

"Thanks, but I can take care of myself."

"I know," Dexter agreed, nodding. "I . . . I'm just sayin' . . ."

"What *are* you sayin'?" Monique asked.

"Uh, nothin'," Dexter said quietly, embarrassed.

"Hey, Dexter!" Deedee called, running toward him. "You got a delivery! And you are gonna *freak!*"

She handed Dexter a slip of paper, and when he read it, his eyes became huge.

Ed drove the Burgermobile into the massive parking lot of the Great Western Forum. Dexter had asked him to come along because the order was too big to be handled by just one person.

There was a basketball game in progress and the

62

parking lot was packed with cars. Both boys were excited about the delivery, and Ed got a little carried away at the wheel, zigzagging the Burgermobile around the parking lot.

"Ed!" Dexter cried. "What're you doin'? You gotta park the burger! Slow down!"

Ed laughed and shouted, "Whoooaaaaa!" as he screeched to a stop just outside the huge building. He and Dexter hopped out, each of them carrying several bags of food from Good Burger.

Inside, Ed and Dexter ran down the tunnel that led to the court, but a burly uniformed security guard stepped in front of them.

"Sorry," the guard said in a low, gravelly voice. "Nobody gets past this door."

"But we got a delivery!" Ed cried.

"You *gotta* let us in!" Dexter cried.

"Not without a pass."

Dexter frowned and stepped forward. "Look, Starsky . . . we're from Good Burger, and we—"

The security guard's eyebrows shot up and his eyes widened. "You guys got *Good Burgers* in those bags? *Gimme* one!"

"Sure, dude," Ed said, pulling a burger from one of the bags and handing it over.

"Now will you let us in?"

"Not . . . yet," the guard said, looking all around carefully. Beads of sweat broke out on his forehead as he leaned toward the boys and said, in a low, desperate whisper, "C'mon, *you* know what I want!"

63

"A massage?" Ed asked.

"No," the guard said. *"Sauce!* Gimme some of Ed's Sauce!"

Ed and Dexter exchanged a glance and Dexter shrugged, reaching into one of the bags. He handed over a small container of sauce, saying, "Okay, here."

"More," the guard said, his hands trembling, sweat dribbling down his face.

"More?" Ed asked.

"Please," the guard begged, "I *need* it . . . *I gotta have it!"* Ed handed him another container. *"More!"* the guard said.

"Man, are you gonna *eat* this stuff," Dexter asked, "or take a *bath* in it?" He shoved two more containers at the guard, then pushed him aside, saying, *"There!* Now get outta the way!"

"Bless you!" the guard cried. He looked around quickly, then ran off to eat his Good Burger with lots of extra sauce.

Ed and Dexter dashed through the unguarded door.

In the locker room, television reporters were gathered around Shaquille O'Neal. Microphones were shoved in his face and television cameras were trained on him.

"So," a reporter asked, "after scoring that *amazing* last-minute game-winning shot and bringing your team all the way to the NBA championship, how do you feel?"

Shaq thought about the question a moment, then said, "I feel . . . *hungry!"*

At that moment, Ed and Dexter burst into the locker room and headed toward the crowd of reporters.

"We're here!" Dexter shouted.

Ed spread his arms and cried, *"Shaaaq!"* as if he'd known Shaq all his life.

Shaq grinned when he saw them, and the reporters stepped aside to let the boys through. Grabbing one of the bags, Shaq pulled out a Good Burger and unwrapped it.

"Aw, man," Shaq said with disappointment as he checked between the buns. "I asked for *tomato* on my Good Burger! There's no *tomato* here!"

"Oh, hang on!" Ed said with a smile. He reached into his pocket and pulled out a dripping tomato slice, grabbed Shaq's burger, opened it, and slapped the tomato slice onto the patty. "There ya go, Shaq," he said, handing the burger back. "Consider yourself toma-toed!"

Shaq looked at Ed for a long moment with a slight frown, taking his burger back. Then he said quietly, "You're not *like* other people, are you?"

"Take a bite, Shaq!" Dexter said. "Try our new Ed's Sauce!"

Shaq took a big bite of his burger, chewed a few times, then grinned, nodding as he muffled, "Mmmm-*mmmm!"*

"You heard it here, folks!" one of the reporters said, spinning around to face a camera. "Shaquille O'Neal . . . a man who enjoys Good Burgers!"

"Hey, Dex," Ed said, elbowing his buddy, "we're on TV!" Ed stepped forward and leaned close to the camera's lens, grinning as he said, "Welcome to Good

Burger, home of the Good Burger, can I take your order?"

Kurt sat behind his desk in his office glaring at Ed and Dexter on his television. As usual, he was flanked by Troy and Griffen. Good Burgers were being passed all around the locker room and players and reporters alike were biting into them. After a moment of chewing, they broke into a chant: "Ed's Sauce! Ed's Sauce! Ed's Sauce! Ed's Sauce!"

"I am *sick* of those pukes!" Kurt shouted, shooting out of his chair. He rounded his desk, crossed the office and punched the television right in the screen. It wobbled a moment, then fell off its stand and sparked as it hit the floor with a loud *whump* and a puff of smoke. *"Hah!"* Kurt blurted. "You're not so fast with the trash talkin' *now,* are ya?"

"You got 'em that time, bro!" Griffen said with a smile.

"Yeah, but, uh . . ." Troy said cautiously, "if you hadn't noticed, Good Burger is *still* in business."

"Well, what are we supposed to *do* about it?" Griffen asked. "Our burgers are already *twice* the size of theirs!"

Kurt's eyes widened and the small, unpleasant smirk became a broad, threatening grin as he went behind his desk again. "Oh, yeah?" he said, punching a button on the intercom console on his desk. *"Kitchen!"*

Two seconds later, the voice of a male Mondo Chef came over the intercom. "Kitchen, here."

"Make our burgers bigger," Kurt demanded.

"Bigger?" the voice asked. "But . . . we're already—"

"Bigger!" Kurt barked. "Okay, bro?" He hit the button again, then began pacing, still grinning maniacally. "Let's see Good Burger go against burgers *three times* the size of theirs!"

"Great," Troy said. "But, uh . . . what about the Ed's Sauce?"

"Well," Kurt said, pacing back and forth, back and forth, "if Kurt can't *steal* Ed's Sauce . . . then Kurt'll just have to get it straight from the *source!*" He stopped pacing and faced Troy and Griffen.

The three of them broke out in laughter . . . mean, nasty laughter.

Chapter 9

The next day, Ed skated to work. He sang as he skated along the sidewalk:

"I'm a duuude . . . She's a dude . . . He's a dude . . . 'Cause we're all duuudes!"

He hopped off the sidewalk to cross the street just as the familiar black Chevy Yukon drove by.

"Whooaaa!" Ed cried, flailing his arms and trying to stop. But he *couldn't* stop!

The Yukon screeched to a halt right in front of Ed, who slammed into it, tumbled up onto the hood and landed with his face smooshed against the windshield, arms and legs splayed in all directions.

Dazed and confused, Ed stared cross-eyed through the glass at Kurt, who was behind the wheel. With his speech garbled because his mouth was pressed against the windshield, Ed said, "Welcome to Good Burger, home of the Good Burger, can I take your order?"

Kurt got out of the Yukon and helped Ed off the hood, brushing off his clothes and asking, "You all right, bro?"

"Hey!" Ed said, still a little wobbly. "I know you! You're the dude from Mondo Burger!"

"Correctomundo," Kurt said with a crooked smile. He held out his hand to shake. "Kurt Bozwell."

"No, no," Ed corrected, shaking Kurt's hand. "I'm *Ed.*"

"Right. Can I give you a lift, Ed?"

"I dunno. I weigh around one fifty."

"Just, uh . . . get in the car, huh?"

Once Ed was inside the Yukon, Kurt began to drive as Ed looked around in total amazement. The interior of the Yukon was *incredible!* It was decked out with an amazing stereo, a phone, a television and VCR, Nintendo . . . *everything!*

Kurt said, "So, let's talk, homes."

"It's *Ed.* Holmes is that Sherlock detective dude."

"Riiight," Kurt said, rolling his eyes.

Ed reached down to the console between the seats and began pushing buttons at random. As he poked at the buttons, music came on, went off, the television came on, went off, a Nintendo game began to play on the screen, then blinked out.

"Whoooaaaa!" Ed said with delight, reaching down to hit another button.

Kurt grabbed his wrist and shouted, "Dude! *Quit* it! Check it out, Ed: *after* we talk, you can push all the buttons you want. Okay?"

"Done deal!" Ed exclaimed with a grin.

"Stellar," Kurt said, letting go of Ed's wrist. "Ed, I'm gonna cut right to the chase. You've been workin' at Good Burger now for, like, three years. And your manager only pays you five bucks an hour."

"Really?" Ed asked, surprised. *"Cool!"*

"Well, if *five* bucks an hour is cool," Kurt said, "how does *ten* bucks sound?"

"Hmmm . . . hang on." Ed pulled a ten dollar bill from his pocket, held it up to his ear and crinkled it up . . . uncrinkled it . . . crinkled it up again. "Uuhhh . . . it sounds sorta like, um . . . well, it's a kinda . . . *chusha-chusha-chusha* sound," he said, stuffing the bill back into his pocket.

Kurt sighed with frustration, clutching the steering wheel hard. "Look, Ed, I want you to bail on Good Burger and come to work for me at Mondo Burger. I want you to make your sauce for *Kurt.*"

"Who's Kurt?" Ed asked.

"I'm Kurt!"

"I'm Ed."

"I'm aware!"

"Oh? I thought you said you were *Kurt!*"

With an angry growl, Kurt took a corner suddenly, drove around the block and screeched to a halt in front of Good Burger. Without looking at Ed, he took in a deep, frustrated breath and let it out in a long, grumbling sigh.

"Thanks for the ride," Ed said pleasantly, getting out of the Yukon.

"Yeah, sure," Kurt said. He turned to Ed and tried to smile, hiding his anger and annoyance. "And when you're ready to work for me, you just say the word."

Ed closed the door, then tapped on the window. It hummed open.

"Yeah?" Kurt said.

"What's the word?" Ed asked.

"Whatever. You pick."

"Okay. The word is . . . *seven!*" Ed said with a grin.

Kurt's face twisted into a grimace as he shifted into gear and sped away in the Yukon.

Dexter jogged out of Good Burger to Ed's side. He did *not* look happy as he asked, *"What* were you doin' in Kurt's car?"

"Pushin' buttons," Ed said. "Talkin' to Kurt."

"What'd he *say* to you?"

"Somethin' about me goin' to work for him at Mondo Burger. He likes me."

"No! He wants your *sauce!* Look, whatever you do, do *not* tell him your sauce recipe! Don't tell *anyone!* Remember, if you tell anyone the recipe, then Good Burger is going to be in *big* trouble!"

"Okay!" Ed agreed happily.

"Okay," Dexter said, starting back toward the entrance to Good Burger. "C'mon, let's get to work."

"Wait!" Ed called, fishing around in his jacket pocket. "I got you somethin'!"

Dexter turned back, curious, as Ed took a yo-yo out of his pocket. He handed it to Dexter, who gazed at it with surprise, and just a little awe. It looked very familiar.

"What's this?" Dexter asked.

"It's a yo-yo!" Ed said, grinning. "I bought it with the thirteen dollars you gave me. See? It lights up and whistles and *everything!* Just like the one your dad gave you."

Dexter stared at the yo-yo for a long moment, then slipped the string on his finger and flipped his hand. The yo-yo lit up—red on one side, blue on the other—as it whistled down the string, then whistled back up again, landing in his palm with a soft *smack*. He stared at the yo-yo in his hand feeling touched . . . and more than a little guilty. He looked at Ed and asked, "Why'd you get this for me?"

Ed said, "Well . . . *cuz!* We're buddies! C'mon, let's go to work!" He skated along the sidewalk and into Good Burger.

Dexter stared at the yo-yo for a moment longer. "Buddies," he said, as a smile grew on his face. "Yeah, I guess we are." Then he turned and went back inside.

During his lunch break, Dexter had to run an errand for his mother, so he took off on his bike. But Ed was still hard at work, handling customers at the counter inside. Good Burger's booths were all taken up by customers happily chowing down on their Good Burgers with Ed's Sauce, but there was no line at the counter for the moment. Ed stood at his post, staring off into space, wondering how mud puddles felt when the tires of cars rolled through them.

A short, balding, middle-aged man walked up to the

72

counter with his Good Burger in hand. He smiled reluctantly as he said, in a very soft voice, "Excuse me . . . this burger is extremely rare."

"What's so special about it?" Ed asked.

"No, no," the man said, holding the burger out for Ed to see. A single bite had been taken from the burger, and the man peeled back the top bun, saying, "Look at the meat. See how pink it is? That's *very* rare."

"No, it's not!" Ed said with a big smile. "We got *tons* more meat in the back just *like* that!"

The man closed his eyes for a moment, took a deep breath, then said, "Look, try to follow me . . ."

"Where are we goin'?"

"We're not going *anywhere,*" the man said, raising his voice a bit.

"Then why'd you invite me?"

"Oh, just . . . *forget* the burger! Just give me a Good Shake."

Ed shrugged, leaned over the counter and grabbed the man's lapels, shaking him vigorously.

"Hey!" the man blurted. "Would you—hey, ooh— just stop with the *shaking!*"

A man holding a clipboard and wearing a blue uniform entered Good Burger and said loudly, "Delivery for . . . uh, Ed?"

Ed let go of the customer's lapels suddenly, and the man dropped to the floor in a surprised heap.

"I'm a Ed!" Ed called, running out from behind the counter to the deliveryman's side.

"There's a gift for you. Outside."

"For *me?*" Ed exclaimed. He followed the delivery-man out of the restaurant.

Meanwhile, Dexter was making his way back to work on his bike. He took all the shortcuts he knew, because he'd been gone a little too long. If he didn't get back soon, he'd be late. As busy as Good Burger had been lately, he couldn't afford to be late, because they needed all the help they could get.

Just a block away from Good Burger, Dexter slowed down a bit . . . and he became aware of a sound beside him . . . a *clippety-cloppety clippety-cloppety* sound. He looked to his right . . . and gasped.

There was a chestnut-colored *horse* beside him . . . and riding that horse was *Ed!*

"What the—" Dexter blurted, swallowing the rest of his sentence. "Ed! What are you *doing?*"

"Ridin' my pony."

"Where did you *get* that *horse?*"

"Kurt gave him to me. Isn't he cute?" Ed asked, petting his horse. "And since he's chestnut colored, I named him . . . *Blueberry!*"

Dexter stopped his bike and got off. Ed and his horse stopped beside him. "Get *down* from that thing!" Dexter shouted.

Ed got off the horse and asked, "Why? Whatcha gonna do?"

"You'll see," Dexter said.

Minutes later, Dexter, Ed, and Blueberry were standing outside Mondo Burger.

"Go open the door," Dexter said, waving toward the front entrance of Mondo Burger.

Ed walked over to the door and held it open as Dexter slapped Blueberry hard on the behind. The horse shot forward and trotted straight into Mondo Burger. Ed let the door go and walked away as it swung closed.

As Ed and Dexter headed across the street to Good Burger, muffled crashing sounds came from inside Mondo Burger. A moment later, customers began to pour out chaotically, screaming and cursing, some of them still holding their giant Mondo Burgers in hand.

Dexter began to laugh, and a moment later, so did Ed. Dexter held the door of Good Burger open and said to Ed, "After you!"

"After me!" Ed said, going inside. Then they began to laugh again.

"What is *with* this dude?" Kurt growled between clenched teeth as he paced furiously back and forth in front of his desk.

He was in his office with Troy and Griffen . . . and Blueberry. Griffen stood in front of the horse, feeding it a handful of French fries.

"He doesn't wanna work at Mondo Burger," Griffen said.

"If you ask *me,*" Troy said, "the guy's a few tacos short of a combination plate."

"I don't *care,*" Kurt grumbled. "Kurt's gonna get his sauce. I didn't come *this* far to let a tired little crap shack like *Good Burger* get in my way!"

Kurt continued to pace as Blueberry gobbled up the fries from Griffen's hand with a lot of wet snuffling sounds. Suddenly, Kurt stopped pacing and went behind his desk. He leaned over and hit a button on the intercom console.

"Bring in Roxanne!" he shouted. Then he punched the button again and stood up straight, grinning. "If *anyone* can get the sauce out of Ed . . . *she* can."

Troy and Griffen grinned along with their boss.

Chapter 10

Standing at his post at the counter, Ed studied the three hamburgers spread out before him.

"Good Burger," he muttered to himself, "old Mondo Burger . . . and *new* Mondo Burger."

Mr. Baily approached him, saying, "Ed, this has *got* to stop."

Ed turned to him, amazed. "But Mondo Burgers are gettin' even *bigger!* See, here's one from last week . . . and here's one I got today. *See?* They're gettin' *huger!*"

"Great," Mr. Baily said. "That's fine. But for now, just worry about our customers, okay?"

Ed turned to see a woman standing at the counter, smiling, and he said, "Welcome to Good Burger, home of the Good Burger, can I take your order?"

"Hello, my name is Connie Muldoon," the woman said. Connie Muldoon spoke rapidly, the words shooting from her mouth like bullets from a machine gun. "I'm hosting a family reunion and my oven has run amok. I think it's the heat actuator. Anyhoo, I would like to order . . ." She studied the menu on the wall above and behind Ed. ". . . three Good Meals, four Junior Good Meals, a seventeen-piece order of your Good Chunks . . . ummm . . . okay, in two of the Junior Good Meals, I want to substitute the Good Cookies for Good Pies—and don't fret if that's extra, I'll pony up the overage—and, uh . . . oh, on the regular Good Meals, I need two of the Good Burgers to have ketchup, mayo, mustard, lettuce, tomato, but no onion—I've got an interview this afternoon—okay, let's see, that covers everyone but Uncle Leslie, who doesn't eat meat, but of course he *does* eat dairy, so I don't get it, um . . . let's get Leslie a Good Chickwich . . . and some Good Fries, and a Good Root Beer . . . all to go, but I would like to have my beverage while I wait. Now. Total me up."

Ed's eyes glazed over as he stared at Connie Muldoon in deep shock.

"Young man?" she said. "What's the total? Time for addition. Hello?"

Ed did not move or make a sound as he stared with crossed eyes, mouth hanging open.

"Oh, dear," Connie Muldoon whispered, looking around cautiously. "I think I broke him." Then she turned and hurried away.

While Ed was staring blankly at nothing in particular, his mind momentarily out of commission after Connie Muldoon's enormous, rapid-fire order, a beautiful girl approached the counter.

"Hello?" the girl said to Ed. "Uh . . . *hello?*"

Ed's vision was blurred, but slowly came back into focus as he stared at the beautiful girl.

She was about eighteen years old . . . and absolutely drop *dead* gorgeous.

Ed shook his head back and forth several times, then said, "Uh . . . welcome to Good Burger, home of the Good Burger, can I take your order?"

"No, thanks," she said with a beautiful smile. "I just came here to meet *you*, Ed. I'm Roxanne."

Dexter walked by behind Ed, but slowed his pace when he noticed Roxanne. He stayed close by, eavesdropping on their conversation.

Ed's mouth worked, but nothing came out in response to what Roxanne had said. Finally, he babbled, "Welcome to Good Burger, home of the Good Burger, can I take your order?"

Roxanne leaned toward him over the counter and whispered, "You are *sooo* hot."

Dexter's mouth dropped open in shock. He snapped it shut again.

"Yeah," Ed said, "I often sweat when I work. So, you hungry?"

Dexter rolled his eyes, amazed by Ed's cluelessness.

"Yes, I *am* hungry," Roxanne said. "But not for food. I'm hungry for *you.*"

Ed's eyebrows popped up. "But . . . I'm not edible."

"How would you like to go out on a date tomorrow night, Ed?"

"Hey, sounds great! With who?"

"*Me,* silly."

79

Ed grinned sheepishly. "Me silly, too."

"No, I meant that you and I should go out together. Tomorrow night. Want to?"

"Uh . . . *sure*. Okay."

"Awesome," she said, flashing that incredible smile again. She handed him a slip of paper saying, "Here's my address. I'll see you at eight." She blew Ed a kiss, gave him a wink, then left Good Burger.

Dexter stepped over to Ed's side, stunned and amazed. "I can't believe what I just saw!" he said.

Ed turned to him, curious. "Elvis?"

"No, not *Elvis!* A beautiful girl just cruised in here and asked you out on a date!"

"I know. Hey, Dex, wanna come with us?"

"Nah," Dexter said. "Three's a crowd."

"So, bring a date," Ed said with a shrug. "Hey, why don't you ask Monique?"

Dexter thought about it a moment, then shook his head. "I . . . I don't think so."

"Why not? You *know* you like her."

"How could I *not* like her?" Dexter asked, glancing at Monique, who was over by the milk shake machine. "I mean, she's smart, funny, beautiful . . . cuddly." A smile grew on his face as he thought about Monique.

"So, ask her out!" Ed prodded.

"No."

"Chicken."

"I'm not a chicken," Dexter said, frowning.

"Are too!" Ed chanted loudly, "Dexter's a chicken! Chicken! Chicken!" Then Ed tucked his thumbs into his

80

armpits, flapped his elbows like wings, tilted his head back and said loudly, *"Moooo! Moooo!"*

"Cut that out!" Dexter snapped. "I am *not* a *chicken!* Look, Monique probably doesn't wanna waste her time goin' out with me, so let's drop it, all *right?"*

Ed stared at him for a moment, then flapped his elbows again and cried, *"Moooo!"*

"And chickens do not *moo!"* Dexter said. "They *cluck!"*

As Monique walked by them, Ed turned to her and said, "Hey, Monique, we're goin' out tomorrow night. You wanna be Dexter's date?"

Dexter cringed with embarrassment as he leaned toward Ed and whispered, "I *told* you I—"

"I'd love to," Monique said with a smile. Then she disappeared into the kitchen.

Dexter stared for a moment at the spot where Monique had stood, then smiled and said, "I knew she'd say yes."

The following night, the four of them went to the Fun Emporium, an enormous complex made up of a video game arcade, a go-cart track, a miniature golf course, and a big food court. Ed drove them there in the Burgermobile. Dexter, Monique, and Roxanne were dressed casually. Ed wore his Good Burger uniform . . . with a tie.

The Fun Emporium was brightly lit and the air was a mixture of delicious food smells, everything from burritos to cotton candy. Ed and Roxanne and Dexter and

81

Monique played video games for a while, then went to a corn dog stand for something to eat. They carried their corn dogs to a small table with four chairs.

"Your chair, madam," Dexter said gallantly as he pulled Monique's chair out for her.

"Why, thank you, Dexter," Monique said as she sat down.

Following Dexter's example, Ed pulled Roxanne's chair out as she started to sit down, saying, "Your chair."

But he pulled it out too far. Roxanne fell flat on her behind with a yelp. Others in the food court turned and stared.

"Whooaaa!" Ed cried. "Is your butt okay?"

Roxanne scrambled to her feet and brushed herself off, forcing a smile. "It's fine, thank you."

When he saw that people were still staring, Ed raised his hands and shouted, "It's okay, people! Her butt is fine!"

Mortified, Roxanne sat down at the table and slumped down in her chair.

"Mmm, great corn dog," Monique said as they all began to eat.

Ed stared at his corn dog and said, "I wonder how they get the weenie inside the corny exterior?"

"A question that's plagued mankind for centuries," Dexter said.

"You know what would go *great* on these corn dogs, Ed?" Roxanne asked, leaning close to him.

"A leotard?" Ed replied.

A moment passed while Dexter, Monique, and Roxanne stared at Ed with confusion.

"No, silly," Roxanne said. "Some of your *sauce*. I just *love* your sauce, Ed. How do you make it? I'm *dying* to know."

"Oh, it's easy. You start off with ketchup, add a little lemon juice, and—"

Dexter kicked hard under the table, meaning to kick Ed . . . but he kicked Roxanne instead.

"Ooowww!" Roxanne cried.

Dexter winced. "Oops."

"What's the matter, Roxanne?" Ed asked. "Is it your butt?"

"No!"

"Uh, whatta you say we start puttin' on the miniature golf course?" Dexter suggested, hoping to smooth things over.

Dexter and Monique quickly finished off their corn dogs and went on to the golf course ahead of Ed and Roxanne. But Ed wasn't far behind them.

"Let's go, Roxanne," he said, getting up from the table.

"Ed . . . can't we go somewhere and be alone?"

Roxanne stepped in front of him and stood very close, playing with his tie as she spoke. "Well . . . maybe we could . . . talk? Maybe we could get to know each other a little better? Now, doesn't that sound like more fun than miniature golf?"

Ed looked deep into her beautiful eyes as he considered her question, then said, "No. C'mon!" He turned and hurried after Dexter and Monique.

Sighing with frustration, Roxanne followed close behind.

At the first hole, Monique went first. She putted the

ball and it rolled directly toward the cup . . . closer . . . closer . . . but it stopped just short of dropping in.

"So close and yet so far," Dexter said, taking her place. "My turn." Dexter putted, and the ball zipped way past the cup.

Monique giggled. "So, this is your first time."

Smirking, Dexter said, "Yeah, keep talkin', just keep talkin'."

"My turn!" Ed called. He put a ball on the tee, grabbed a putter and settled into position. He stretched first one arm, then the other. Then he stuck out his butt, wiggled his hips back and forth as he shifted his weight back and forth from one foot to the other, back and forth. He rolled his head loosely on his neck, scraped his shoes on the AstroTurf-covered concrete, cleared his throat, wiggled his butt some more . . .

Dexter rolled his eyes as Monique giggled into her palm.

Looking very impatient, Roxanne stepped forward just as Ed was about to swing. "Ed, can't we just—" she began, but before she could finish, Ed's backswing smacked her right in the face. She fell flat on her back with an ugly grunt.

Ed followed through, shouting, "Fore!" and sent the ball whizzing through the air. It hit one of the rotors on the windmill and began to ricochet wildly!

With a pained groan, Roxanne clambered to her feet, rubbing her sore face.

The ball continued to ricochet madly, making its way around them, and it would've come right back to Ed from behind . . . if Roxanne had not been in the way. Instead, the ball nailed her on the back of the head, and she fell flat on her face with another grunt.

The golf ball bounced over to Ed's feet. He picked it up, then went to Roxanne's side, leaned down, and said, "Your turn!"

Ten minutes later, they were all back in the Burgermobile, having decided to cut their evening short. Dexter sat in the backseat with his arm around Monique's shoulders. Roxanne sat up front with Ed, who drove as he told her his life story, which seemed even longer than his life.

"Then," Ed continued, "when I was six, I said my very first word. My mom thinks it was 'trousers,' but I'm pretty sure it was 'tweezers.' Anyway, when I was nine, I went to summer camp. I'll never forget—"

"Ed?" Dexter said. "She's still unconscious, man."

Ed turned to Roxanne. Sure enough, she was still out cold.

Ed said, "Uuuhhh . . . no?"

A few minutes later, with Roxanne still unconscious beside him, Ed drove the Burgermobile into the parking lot of Good Burger and pulled *verrrry slooowly* and *verrrry caaarefully* into a parking space. Then he *pounded* his foot onto the brake pedal, bringing the car to a sudden, grinding halt.

Roxanne flew forward in her seat and slammed her head against the dashboard. She sat up suddenly, sputtering and wincing.

"That woke her up!" Ed said happily.

"What happened?" Roxanne asked.

Ed explained, "Your head hit my golf ball . . . then you went sleepy-bye."

She felt her head and face and groaned in pain, but quickly pulled herself together, giving Ed another forced smile.

In the backseat, Dexter asked, "Uh, Monique, you wanna take a walk?"

"Sure," she said.

"Hey, wait!" Ed said over his shoulder. "What am *I* supposed to do?"

Roxanne cleared her throat loudly and said, "Uh, *hello?*"

Ed smiled at her, said, "Hello," then turned back to Dexter. "So, what am *I* supposed to do?"

As she got out of the car with Dexter, Monique said with a wink, "I'm sure Roxanne will help you figure *something* out."

Dexter and Monique got out of the Burgermobile and walked slowly across the parking lot together.

"Are you cold?" Dexter asked.

"What tipped you off? Was it the shivering, or my chattering teeth?"

"Actually, it was that big icicle growing on your butt," Dexter said, taking off his jacket. He put it around her shoulders. As they walked on, Monique took Dexter's hand, which surprised him just a little. "So, uh, you like me?" he asked.

"Of course," she replied, smiling. "So, uh . . . you like me?"

"You kiddin'? I liked you the first day I saw you. Right off the bat. I guess it was the same way for you, too, huh?"

"Actually," Monique said, "I thought you self-centered and obnoxious."

"Ah. Well, so much for my self-esteem."

"I changed my mind, though, didn't I?"

"Yeah," Dexter said. "How come?"

"Ed."

" 'Scuse me?"

"Ed thinks you're a really great guy. He always talks about what a good friend you are to him, and about what a nice, caring person you are."

"Really? He said all that?" Dexter asked. He turned his head so Monique couldn't see him wince as he thought about his "contract" with Ed.

"Yeah," Monique said. "Ed is the sweetest, most genuine person I've ever met." She stopped walking and turned to face Dexter. "Anyone he likes so much can't be all bad." She leaned forward and gave him a long, warm kiss.

Dexter would have enjoyed it a lot more if he weren't so preoccupied with the lump of guilt in his chest.

Meanwhile, Ed and Roxanne had gotten out of the Burgermobile and were leaning against the side of the car together.

"So, Ed," Roxanne said, taking Ed's hand, "what do you want to do?"

"Well . . . I've always wanted to shave a possum!" Ed replied.

Roxanne closed her eyes a moment, trying to contain her frustration. Then she smiled and said, "I mean . . . what do you want to do with *me?*"

"Well, I guess I could shave a possum with you," Ed said. He let go of her hand, reached into his pocket and pulled out a disposable razor. "Got a possum?"

Roxanne took the razor from his hand and tossed it over her shoulder as she stepped in front of him. "Look at me, Ed."

"I'm lookin'," he said.

"What do you see?"

"Uh . . . I see a red lump on your forehead where the golf club hit you."

"Look into my *eyes*, Ed."

Ed's eyes widened as he stared deeply into Roxanne's. She leaned so close to him that their faces were almost touching.

"Ed?" she whispered in a breathy, sexy voice. "Tell me how you make your sauce . . . and I will give you *anything* you want."

"Whatcha got?" Ed asked.

"For starters? How about . . . *this.*" Roxanne threw her arms around Ed to kiss him, but before their lips touched, Ed reacted instinctively.

He grabbed her arm and Judo-flipped her onto her back with a thud.

"Sorry!" Ed exclaimed. "But . . . you *surprised* me!"

Roxanne lay on her back, cross-eyed and groaning.

The next morning, Roxanne hobbled into Kurt's office on crutches. She wore a bandage on her forehead, a sling on her arm, her hair was a mess, and she was *furious*.

"I *quit!*" she shouted, just before tripping over her own crutches and falling on her face.

Kurt sat behind his desk, flanked, as usual, by Troy and Griffen.

"I'm guessing," Griffen said, "she didn't get the sauce recipe."

"I am *aware*," Kurt growled. He clenched his fists, wondering if he would *ever* be able to get the recipe for Good Burger's hugely successful sauce.

Chapter 11

The next day, Dexter entered Good Burger's back door and went to his locker in the employee changing area. He stopped when he saw Monique putting her purse in her locker.

Otis sat on a stool against the wall, sound asleep and snoring quietly.

Dexter sneaked up behind Monique, reached around and covered her eyes with his hands, saying, "Guess who?"

She reached up and pulled his hands away, then turned and backed away from him a couple steps. "Hi, Dexter," she said coldly.

"Whatcha doin'?" he asked.

"Getting ready for work."

"Well, um, listen, Monique . . . I thought, y'know, since we had such a good time last night and all, that maybe you'd wanna go out again tonight?"

"I don't think so," she said. The warmth that had been in her voice the night before was gone.

"Oh. Okay, then . . . tomorrow night?"

"No."

Dexter frowned and scratched his head, wondering why Monique was being so unfriendly. "Uh . . . maybe this weekend, then?"

"Maybe not."

"Okay. Who *are* you and what have you done with the *real* Monique?" Dexter asked, expecting a laugh. He didn't get one.

"She's right here," Monique said. "It's just that now, she knows the *real* Dexter."

"Come again?"

Monique removed Dexter's jacket from her locker and handed it to him, saying, "You forgot your jacket last night."

"Oh, yeah," Dexter said, hooking two fingers under the jacket's collar and dangling it over his shoulder.

Monique removed a folded piece of paper from her locker. *"This* fell out of the pocket," she said, handing it to Dexter.

When he unfolded the paper, his eyes widened. It was his "contract" with Ed. "Oh, uh . . . this is . . . well, this is just . . ."

"It's the contract you had Ed sign," Monique said angrily. "You know, the one where *you* take most of the money *he's* supposed to get for *his* sauce."

"Ooohhh, yeah, uh . . ." Dexter tried to think fast. "Well, y'know, this is just—"

"I can't *believe* you would do something like that to

9 1

someone who *trusts* you, Dexter," Monique said, folding her arms tightly over her chest. "How could you take advantage of a sweet person like Ed? And after he got you a *job!*"

Dexter dropped his coat on a nearby bench and waved his hands, saying, "No, no, it's not like that! I only wanted—"

"I *know* what you wanted, Dexter. You're not Ed's friend. You're just *using* him to scam a little cash on the side. Must feel pretty good, huh?" She turned to leave, but stopped and faced him again, arms still folded. "Oh, and don't worry, Dexter. I'm not gonna tell Ed you're cheating him."

"Why not?"

"Because it would hurt him too much," she said quietly. Then she spun around and stalked out of the room angrily.

Dexter sighed heavily, running a hand down over his face hard. He turned and saw that Otis was awake now, watching him.

"Punk," Otis said. Then he got off the stool and followed Monique out . . . only a *lot* slower.

With shoulders slumped dejectedly, Dexter went to his locker and opened it. He removed the yo-yo Ed had given him, looped the string around a finger, and snapped his wrist downward. The yo-yo lit up and whistled as it spun downward, then upward again . . . downward and then upward . . . flashing and whistling. It was *exactly* like the one his dad had given him when he was a little kid . . . and Ed had been the only person he'd known since then who was thoughtful enough to buy him another. And he'd bought it with the little bit of money he'd had left after handing most of his earnings over to Dexter.

Staring at the yo-yo in his hand, Dexter shook his head and sighed, feeling terribly sad about how he'd treated his friend Ed.

Later that morning, Ed went out the back door to dump some trash into the Dumpster. But as soon as he was done, he sat down on the back steps where he'd left the two hamburgers he'd been inspecting for so long: one Good Burger and one Mondo Burger. Frowning, trying to concentrate, he held one in each hand, weighing them against one another.

It just didn't make sense. Good Burgers were the same as they'd always been . . . but *somehow,* Mondo Burgers had become *three times* the size of Good Burgers, and they *still* sold for the same price. Ed knew there had to be some secret to it . . . but what *was* that secret?

As he continued comparing the two burgers, Dexter came around the corner of the building.

"There ya are," Dexter said. "Mind if I sit there?"

"On my lap?"

"No, Ed. I'll just, y'know, sit next to you here." Dexter seated himself on the back steps next to Ed. He thought for a long moment, frowning, chewing on his lower lip, trying to find the right words. Finally, he said, "Ed, um . . . how do I say this?"

Ed turned to him and smiled, saying, "It's easy! You just go, *'thiiisss'!"*

"No, no . . . put the burgers down," Dexter said,

removing the contract from his pocket. "I wanna talk to you about this . . . this contract. Y'see, when I had you sign this, I really didn't *mean* to—"

Dexter was interrupted by the barking of a dog. He turned to see a scraggly stray running toward them. The dog stopped in front of them and barked at Ed.

"Uh-oh!" Ed said. "What is it, boy?"

The dog barked a few more times, hopping around excitedly.

"Oh, *no!*" Ed cried. "Four clowns? In *trouble?*"

"Ed . . ." Dexter said, trying not to sound impatient.

The dog barked some more, pawing at Ed's legs.

"Their *car* broke down?" Ed went on. "Oh, *no!* That's *terrible!*"

"Ed, I don't think that—"

"Hang on, Dex!" Ed said. "This dog's trying to tell us that four clowns are stuck somewhere with a broken-down car!" He turned to the dog again and leaned forward, still holding a hamburger in each hand. "Where, boy? Where are the clowns?"

"Ed . . . there are no *clowns,*" Dexter said. "The dog's just hungry."

"He is?" Ed asked, sitting up straight. He looked down at the hamburgers in his hands. "Ooohhh! Well, we should *feed* him!" Ed put the Good Burger on his lap and opened up the Mondo Burger. "Hey, boy!" he said to the dog. "I got somethin' for ya! Here . . . have a Mondo Burger!" He took the enormous beef patty from the Mondo Burger and tossed it to the dog.

The patty hit the concrete with a *smack.* The dog

94

rushed over to the patty and sniffed it, jerked its head back and walked away, returning to Ed's feet.

"Whassamatter, boy?" Ed asked. "That's a big beef patty over there!"

The dog started barking again.

"He's talkin' about the clowns again," Ed said, turning to Dexter. "How come he won't eat the Mondo Burger patty?"

"That's a good question," Dexter said. He was suddenly *very* interested in the dog's reaction to the Mondo Burger patty.

"Here, puppy," Ed said, opening the Good Burger. "Here, try a Good Burger patty." He tossed the beef patty.

The dog gobbled it up a second after it hit the ground.

"Would you look at *that!*" Dexter said.

"See, Dex? *Told* ya! I *told* ya somethin's weird about Mondo Burgers!" He pointed to the dog, saying, *"He* knows somethin's wrong! *Don'tcha,* boy?"

The dog stood up on its hind legs and barked frantically at Ed.

"No, no," Ed said to the dog. "I'm not talkin' about the *clowns,* I'm talkin' about the *Mondo* Burger!"

"You may be right, Ed," Dexter said. He left the steps, went over to the Mondo Burger patty, leaned down and picked it up. "C'mere, boy! *Here,* boy!"

The dog hurried over to Dexter and sniffed the patty he was offering. Again, the dog jerked its head back and scurried away, returning to Ed and barking some more.

"He definitely senses somethin' he doesn't like," Dexter said, dropping the patty.

"What do you think it could be, Dex?"

"I don't know," Dexter said. "How would you like to find out?"

Dexter and Ed exchanged a smiling, mischievous look.

"I've got an idea," Dexter said. "C'mon, let's go!"

They hurried away, leaving the dog alone. Once the boys were out of sight, the dog sat on the concrete and whined.

Thirty-two miles away, on a lonely and deserted stretch of highway, a car stood on the shoulder. Its hood was up and steam billowed upward from the radiator. Four clowns stood around the car in brightly colored, over-size clothes and huge shoes.

One of the clowns paced back and forth in front of the car. His giant, floppy shoes made slapping noises against the pavement with each step he took.

Slap-slap. Slap-slap.

"Where *is* that stupid *dog?*" he shouted.

When the other three clowns shrugged silently, he continued pacing.

Slap-slap. Slap-slap. Slap-slap.

Chapter 12

Later that afternoon, Mondo Burger was busy . . . but not as busy as it had been when it first opened. Even though Mondo Burgers were now three times the size of Good Burgers, and sold for the same price, they could not draw the kind of crowds that filled Good Burger . . . because they didn't have Ed's Sauce on them. The crowds gathered at Good Burger not because the burgers were huge . . . but because they had *Ed's Sauce!*

As the Mondo Burger employees waited on their customers . . . and as customers took their burgers to booths and settled down to eat . . . two hunched-over little old ladies hobbled through Mondo Burger's front entrance. They took a few steps into the restaurant as the door swung closed behind them, then lifted their heads to look around.

The little old ladies were Ed and Dexter!

Ed wore a blond wig with bangs and a bun on top

and a purple scarf tied around it. His dress was a bizarre red and blue and hot pink print; he wore a red and orange scarf around his neck and carried a leopard-skin purse.

Dexter wore a bobbed wig of brown hair and a narrow-brimmed black hat with some red feathers sticking up on the side. There were red gloves on his hands and he carried a red purse. He wore a yellow-based batik skirt and matching blouse, and a bright lime-green scarf around his neck.

Both boys wore dangly earrings and sensible shoes— *very* sensible—and stood arm-in-arm, looking around the restaurant.

"Dexter?" Ed said. "I'm not, uh . . . comfortable."

"Shhh!" Dexter hissed. "Don't speak, okay? Just come with me."

They shuffled away from the front entrance together, heads slightly bowed, trying to be nonchalant and invisible.

"C'mon," Dexter whispered, "over there . . . down that hallway."

They headed down a hallway to the side of the front counter. Dexter knew, from his *very* short time as a Mondo Burger employee, that it led to the kitchen . . . and *that* was where they wanted to go.

They were halfway down the hallway when a burly Mondo Burger employee stepped in front of them. He was tall *and* wide, with a thick neck. A paper Mondo Burger cap was perched atop his bald head.

"Excuse me, ladies," he said. "May I help you?"

In a quavering, little-old-lady voice, Dexter said, "Oh,

we're just looking for the ladies' rest room, that's all, son."

"Yeah," Ed said in his regular voice. "We gotta *tinkle!*"

The Mondo Burger man frowned at Ed as Dexter squeezed Ed's arm, trying to tell him to shut *up.*

"Oh, don't mind her," Dexter said. "She's always had a deep voice. Started smoking when she was just a girl way back in nineteen aught seven." He turned to Ed and said, "Just *hush* your mouth up, baby."

Ed said, again in his regular voice, "Uh, sorry."

Dexter shot Ed an angry look that said, without words, *Would you just shut up!*

"I said *hush,* dear!" Dexter said to Ed, squeezing his arm again. "Now, let's get on to the little girls' room."

"Uh, ma'am," the Mondo Burger man said, "the rest rooms are over there on the other side of the restaurant. I'll show you."

He took Dexter's free arm and turned him around, starting to lead him back down the hallway.

"Hey, now!" Dexter said, in his old lady voice. "Get your *hands* off me! You *pre-vert,* you!" Dexter tilted his head back and cried, *"Help* me! Oh! I'm an old woman bein' harassed by a mighty man!"

The Mondo Burger man let go of his arm immediately, eyes wide with alarm. "Ma'am, I was just trying to—"

"Ack!" Dexter cried as he fell back against the wall. He flailed his arms and gasped for breath, making gurgling sounds in his throat. "Ooohhh!" he cried in a thin, strangled voice. "Water! Waaaater! Ooohhh!"

Ed turned to him, panicking, and said, "You want me to get you some wa—"

Dexter's flailing hand just *happened* to slap Ed right in the mouth.

"Shut *up!*" Dexter hissed through clenched teeth. Turning back to the Mondo Burger man, he made an ugly gurgling sound in his throat. "Gurrggllle! Water! Please! Water! Hurry!"

The Mondo Burger man stepped forward and looked at Dexter with great concern. "Water? Yes, ma'am! Be right back!"

He turned and jogged down the hallway toward the restaurant.

Dexter stood up straight and turned to Ed. "Don't you know when you're bein' told to *shut up?*"

Ed said, "Uuuhhhh . . . no?"

"C'mon," Dexter said quietly, "let's *go!*"

"But what about your water?" Ed asked.

"Oh, will you just—" Dexter grabbed Ed's shoulders, turned him around and pushed him down the hallway, following right behind.

They hurried down the hallway, ducked to the left through a door, and into the kitchen.

It was a huge kitchen, bustling with activity. Workers scurried around frantically, dropping hot fruit pies into their cardboard containers, dipping onion rings and zucchini slices into batter and then deep-frying them, preparing salads. They worked as stiffly and efficiently as robots, and they were all so busy with what they were doing that they didn't notice the two little old ladies who hurried along the edges of the kitchen, silent and hunched over.

But there was a loud rumbling noise in the kitchen, a great electronic hum.

Dexter spotted a long rectangular table. He clutched Ed's arm and pulled him under the table. They hunched there together, watching the activity around them.

The hum was coming from a conveyor belt that stretched out several feet, ending at a chute that connected directly to the grill.

Workers placed beef patties on the conveyor belt at one end. They made their slow, steady way along . . . until another worker dipped an eyedropper into a canister and applied exactly two drops of liquid to each beef patty as it passed, one after another.

The patties were carried along on the conveyor belt, until they disappeared into the chute that opened over the grill. And they dropped through that chute onto the grill *three times bigger* than they'd been at the other end!

"What're those drops they're puttin' in the meat?" Ed whispered, eyes wide with amazement.

"I don't know," Dexter replied. "But I bet *that's* what's makin' those burgers grow so big."

"Cool!" Ed said. *"We* should get some! For Good Burger!"

"No!" Dexter whispered. "That kinda stuff has *got* to be illegal!"

"It *is* illegal," said a voice behind them.

They looked over their shoulders to see Kurt Bozwell leaning down and glaring at them under the table.

Suddenly, hands reached under the table and dragged them out, stood them up, and pushed them against the wall. Two tough-looking thugs glared at them as Kurt grinned.

"Triampathol is *way* illegal," Kurt said. "But it sure makes burgers nice and enormo, doesn't it?"

"Yeah," Dexter said, pressed against the wall by a thug, "but what kind of effect does that stuff have on people when they *eat* your 'enormo' burgers, huh? I mean, what does it *do* to 'em?"

"Uh-oh, ladies," Kurt said, raising both hands and grinning. "Don't *care!*"

Kurt laughed loudly, and the two thugs holding Ed and Dexter against the wall joined in, guffawing like a couple of donkeys.

Suddenly, the two thugs tore off Ed and Dexter's dresses, guffawing the whole time, and tossed the ripped material aside

Stripped of his dress, Dexter wore a T-shirt and a pair of shorts . . . along with his wrinkled stockings and shoes.

Ed, on the other hand, was left wearing lingerie . . . along with the wrinkled stockings and shoes.

Kurt and his thugs burst into gut-busting laughter.

"Yeah, laugh it up, guys," Dexter said. "When people find out you're usin' that illegal junk in your burgers, you're gonna end up in *jail!*" He turned to Kurt and added, "Bro!"

"And that's why nobody outside of this kitchen is gonna find out about it," Kurt said.

"Oh," Dexter snapped back, "and I suppose you think we're just gonna keep our mouths shut?"

"No, not at all," Kurt said. *"I'm* gonna keep your mouths shut!"

A moment later, Dexter suddenly became a burst of energy, flailing his arms and kicking his legs. The thug holding him against the wall was caught off-guard and Dexter broke loose. He plowed into the other thug, the guy holding Ed against the wall. Dexter slammed the thug hard enough to knock him several steps backward and away from Ed.

"Run, Ed!" Dexter shouted. *"Run!"*

"Okay!" Ed began to run *immediately*. And he ran straight into a wall, hitting it so hard that he fell onto his back.

The two thugs grabbed Dexter and Ed immediately. They wrestled them over to Kurt and turned them to face him.

Kurt approached Ed slowly, saying, "Okay, hot shot. I'm tired of playin' games with you, okay? I wanna know what's in your sauce . . . and I wanna know *now!"*

"Forget it!" Dexter shouted, held in the grip of Kurt's muscular thug. "You're *never* getting Ed's Sauce!"

Kurt ignored Dexter and stepped in front of Ed, leaning close . . . *very* close . . . right in Ed's *face.*

In a low, threatening voice, Kurt said, "I want . . . to know . . . what's in . . . your *sauce,* Ed."

Ed's face slowly twisted into a grimace. "Dude," he said. "You *really* need a Tic Tac!"

"Hah-*hah!"* Dexter laughed defiantly.

"That coils it," Kurt growled through clenched teeth. "You guys are *grass* . . . and *I* am a Snapper lawn mower!"

"Whatta you want us to do with 'em?" asked the thug holding Dexter.

"Well, I think it's time to get our friend *Wade* on the phone," Kurt said with a chuckle.

"At Demented Hills?" Troy asked.

"Yes," Kurt said, nodding. "Demented Hills." He grinned at Ed and Dexter. "You boys are going away. *Way* away. For a *looong* time." Then Kurt burst into loud and unpleasant laughter.

Chapter 13

Demented Hills was a sprawling, ominous-looking building atop a grassy hill on the edge of town. In the dark of night, the building looked like a gigantic beast hunkering on the hill, its windows glowing like multiple eyes as it waited to pounce on something . . . or someone.

A white van drove along the narrow road that wound up the hill and ended in the parking lot in front of Demented Hills. Painted on the side of the van was a sillhouette of the enormous hospital. Next to that were the words:

DEMENTED HILLS ASYLUM

Restricting the Disturbed

Since 1922

The van drove across the parking lot and stopped at the institution's yawning entrance. Two men in white uniforms got out, went to the back of the van, opened the doors, and pulled out Ed and Dexter. They were both wearing straitjackets. Handling the boys roughly, the two attendants took them inside the building.

"Whoooaaa!" Ed said as they entered the building's high-ceilinged foyer. "Cool place!"

Ed and Dexter were shoved over to the front desk. Behind it stood a man with a sour-looking face. He looked like he'd just bitten into a lemon. Like the two attendants, he wore a white uniform. A nametag on his breast pocket read HI! I'M WADE.

"Here's your delivery from Good Burger," one of the attendants said.

The other attendant added, "Kurt wants these guys outta sight . . . for a long time."

Wade's mouth curled into something that looked like it was *supposed* to be a smile as he said, "Yeah . . . these guys look *way* disturbed to me. Downright twisted. We better hold 'em here for extended . . . *observation*." Wade laughed quietly, and the two attendants joined in.

"Man, you'd better let us *outta* these things!" Dexter said.

"Sure, not a problem." Wade nodded to the attendants. "Take off their straitjackets."

The man next to Dexter began unfastening the straitjacket's straps and helping him out of it. The other started to help Ed as well, but Ed stepped away from him.

"No, thanks," Ed said. "I can get out of this myself."

While the others looked at Ed as if he were crazy, he

106

closed his eyes tightly, bunched up his face and slammed himself back against the wall hard. There was a horrible *crunch* sound . . . the sound of Ed's shoulder dislocating! *"Yaaaagggghhh!"* Ed bellowed as beads of sweat broke out on his face. He wriggled and twisted and bent and leaned, until . . . he slipped the straitjacket off. He slammed his back against the wall again, and there was *another* horrible *crunch* sound . . . the sound of Ed's shoulder *re*-locating!

Dexter, Wade, and the two attendants gawked at Ed, horrified.

"Whew!" Ed sighed, wiping a hand over his sweaty face. Then he handed the straitjacket over to the attendant and smiled, saying, "I saw it in *Lethal Weapon.*"

Wade shuddered in disgust and said, "Take 'em to their room."

"Our *room?*" Dexter snapped as the attendants led them away. "You can't do that! You can't just *keep* us here! That's illegal! That . . . that's *kidnapping!*"

"I don't think that's what they call it here, Dex," Ed said as they were taken down a long corridor.

Dexter rolled his eyes.

They were thrown into a small room with padded walls, and the door was slammed behind them. One of the attendants peered in through a little square window in the door.

"Don't worry," he said. "Later, we'll let you spend a little time in the recreation room."

Then a heavy lock was thrown with a loud *kuh-chunk,* and the attendants were gone.

Dexter went to the door and began to pound on it,

shouting, "Open this door! I'm not gonna tell you again, dude! Uh, hello?" There was no response. "Okay, I *will* tell you again! Open this door!" Finally, he stopped pounding, turned around, and leaned his back against the door, groaning with frustration.

"Hey, Dex!" Ed exclaimed. "Look! The walls are padded! Look what I can do!" He ran across the room and slammed into the wall, bounced off, slammed into another wall, bounced off, again and again. The whole time, he cried, "Wheee! Whooaaa, cool! Uh . . . ow. *Wheeee!*"

Dexter rolled his eyes and leaned his head back against the door, wondering how they were *ever* gonna get out of Demented Hills.

It was near closing time at Good Burger, but customers were still lining up at the counter for burgers with plenty of Ed's Sauce. But the Good Burger gang, though still polite to their customers, were not smiling.

Ed and Dexter had not been seen since early that day, and everyone was concerned about them. Somehow, the restaurant just didn't feel the same without the sound of Ed calling out, "Welcome to Good Burger, home of the Good Burger, can I take your order?" or singing, "I'm a duuuude . . . *he's* a dude, *she's* a dude, 'Cause we're *all* duuudes!"

Mr. Baily came out of his office, where he had been making phone calls, trying to track down Ed and Dexter. He was frowning as he approached Fizz and Monique, who stood behind the counter.

"Nobody's seen them," Mr. Baily said. "Nobody's heard from them, either." He shook his head and sighed.

"I'm really worried," Monique said, chewing a nail nervously.

"Me, too," Fizz added.

Behind them, asleep on his stool beside the doorway to the kitchen, Otis snored.

The recreation room at Demented Hills had shelves of coloring books and crayons, jigsaw puzzles and board games, stuffed toys and lumps of Play-Doh, a television, a stereo, lots of things to keep the inmates occupied. Two security guards stood just inside the doorway of the room.

Ed sat on a bench against the wall, trying to stick a square wooden peg into a round hole in a bright blue tray.

"Hi."

Ed looked up to see a small, cute teenage girl standing before him, smiling.

"Hi," Ed said, returning her smile. He set the tray and pegs aside.

"My name's Heather," she said, sitting next to him. "I'm a psychopath."

"I'm Ed."

"Have small space aliens ever landed in your brain and told you to break into the zoo and free all the kangaroos, Ed?"

"Not that I recall."

She smiled again. "Do you think I'm cute?"

109

"Sure."

"What's cute about me?"

"Uh, I dunno. Your head?"

"You've got a cute head, too, Ed."

He grinned proudly. "I try to keep it nice. So, whatcha doin' in here?"

"I got in trouble for breaking into the zoo and freeing all the kangaroos."

"Aahhh," Ed said, nodding.

"I like you, Ed," Heather said.

Ed was about to respond when a nurse stepped up to them and said, "Heather, isn't it time for your injection?"

"I hope so," Heather replied with a bright smile.

Across the room, Dexter was playing cards with a little man with frizzy hair and thick glasses. Another man kept reaching across the table and poking Dexter in the chest with his forefinger.

"Go fish," Dexter said wearily.

The little man pulled a card from the deck, looked at it . . . then crumpled it up in his mouth and began to chew.

"Would ya stop eatin' the cards!" Dexter snapped. "And *you* quit *pokin'* me, dude, it's gettin' annoyin'!"

Ed wandered past Dexter and his card game and sat down on another bench beside a *huge* man in a strait-jacket. The man's forehead was small, and his *eyes* were very tiny. His nose was flat and broad, and his lips pulled back over the few teeth he had left in his mouth. He was enormous, with broad shoulders, a muscular neck, and legs like tree trunks. He stared at nothing in particular as

110

he made a low growling sound in his chest. Spittle dribbled down his chin from his mouth.

"Hey," Ed said, "they lent me a jacket just like that one earlier today."

The man's head turned slowly until his beady eyes were locked on Ed. Suddenly, he began to struggle in the straitjacket, growling furiously and slobbering like an animal.

"Hey, dude, *chill*," Ed said. He stood and stepped in front of the big scary man, saying, "Here, lemme help you with that." Ed unfastened the straps one at a time, then stepped back and smiled. "There ya go, dude!"

The huge man shot to his feet, growling again, and pulled the straitjacket off.

When the security guards saw that the frightening man was free, they turned and ran out of the room.

With a frightening grin, the huge man turned and stomped out of the recreation room, his hands curled into claws at his sides.

Smiling, feeling good that he could help someone, Ed walked over to a poster on the wall and read it out loud to himself slowly. "Today . . . is the first day . . . of the rest of your life."

Suddenly, outside the door, there was a terrible crashing sound! Glass shattered and metal clanged onto the tile floor. People began to scream in high-pitched terrified voices. Ed spun around and stared at the recreation room door.

"He's *loose!*" a man cried. *"Aauuuggghh!* Look out!"

"Support! *Support!* We need support over here right away."

"Not the face! No, *pleeaaase,* not the *faaace!*"

Ed shook his head and muttered, "They sure do know how to party around here." Then he continued wandering around the room.

With Ed and Dexter locked away in Demented Hills, Kurt went over to Good Burger in the middle of the night, accompanied by Troy and Griffen. They were all dressed in black and carried small flashlights and shiny metal containers. They picked the lock on the back door of Good Burger and went inside.

It was pitch dark in the back room until they turned on their flashlights. They made their way to the kitchen silently.

"There's the 'fridge," Kurt whispered. "Get the sauce, dudes."

Troy and Griffen opened the large industrial refrigerator and removed two huge pots of Ed's Sauce.

"Got it," Troy said, as he and Griffen put the pots onto the counter. They removed the lids and looked inside.

"Yep," Griffen whispered. "This is it."

"Okay, c'mon, you guys, hurry it up!" Kurt hissed.

They removed the caps from the metal containers and began pouring white powder into both pots of Ed's Sauce.

A frail, hunched-over figure stepped up behind them and looked over their shoulders, asking casually, "What's goin' on in here?"

Kurt, Troy, and Griffen spun around with a jump,

yowling like frightened children. They turned their flashlights on the figure behind them . . . a droopy, sad-looking old man.

It was Otis!

"Stop wavin' that dang light in my face!" Otis barked.

"Who's there?" Kurt asked.

Otis grumbled, "Your momma. Who are you?"

"Relax," Troy said with relief. "It's just the old guy who works here."

"What are you doin' here this late, old man?" Kurt asked.

"I was sleepin' . . . till you woke my butt up." Otis eyed the metal containers they held. "What's that junk you're pourin' into our sauce?"

"Shut up, old man," Troy said.

"Heeyyy," Kurt said mockingly, "don't be rude to the elderly. The old man asked us a question." Kurt held one of the containers up in front of Otis's face. "It's shark venom. And it's gonna make all your little Good Burger customers very, very sick."

"So sick," Troy added, "that I doubt anybody'll ever want to eat here again."

Otis narrowed his eyes as he glared at them, then said, "I'm callin' the police." He turned and headed for the phone, but Griffen grabbed his elbow and turned him around again.

Kurt said, "You're not callin' anyone."

Later that night, as Ed and Dexter lay on their cots in their padded room, unable to sleep, the lock was pulled on the door. The door burst open and a straitjacketed figure was thrown into the room, then the door was slammed and locked again.

Ed and Dexter dove from their cots.

"Otis!" Dexter cried when he recognized the old man. Otis had a gag in his mouth.

"You came to visit!" Ed said happily.

They helped Otis sit up and lean back against the wall.

"Mmmnnmmm! Glmmm-blmmmnnn!" Otis garbled beneath the gag.

"Oh, nothin' much," Ed said. "How *you* been?"

"Just help me get him *out* of this, Ed!" Dexter snapped.

They loosened the straitjacket and pulled it off, then removed the gag from Otis's mouth.

"Do I *look* like I came here to *visit?*" Otis growled at Ed. He looked around. "Where am I? What's going *on?*"

"They kidnapped us," Dexter replied. "But why'd they bring *you* here?"

"'Cause I caught those little Mondo Burger brats dumpin' *shark venom* into our sauce!"

"Shark venom?" Dexter blurted, horrified.

Ed frowned. "But . . . who would wanna harm innocent sharks?"

"Forget the *sharks,*" Dexter said, slapping Ed's shoulder. "That stuff's gonna harm innocent *people!* We gotta make sure no one eats that sauce."

"Can you get to a phone?" Otis asked.

Dexter shook his head. "Not a chance. We gotta get outta this place. What time is it?"

"I'll tell ya!" Ed said. He looked at his wristwatch. And

114

looked . . . and looked. He studied the watch for a long time with a frown of intense concentration.

"Oh, brother," Otis grumbled, looking at his own watch. "It's six A.M., Dexter. Good Burger opens in four hours. But how are we gonna get outta *here?*"

Dexter stroked his chin thoughtfully. "You let me handle that. I think I got an idea."

After a moment of silence, Ed announced proudly, "It's six A.M.!"

Dexter and Otis rolled their eyes.

Chapter 14

The next morning, Ed, Dexter, and Otis sat at a table in the recreation room, working on a jigsaw puzzle. Heather stood behind Ed, watching. As usual, two security guards stood just inside the door, watching as other inmates wandered around the room, some talking to one another, some talking to themselves. Every now and then, a young man sitting in the corner would shoot his fist into the air and shout, "Cry *cheeble!* And let *loose* the hamsters of war!"

"Good morning, patients," said a silver-haired doctor as he walked with a clipboard tucked under his arm. He looked around, smiling at the patients. "I trust you're all getting the day off to a *positive* start. As you know, it's medication time."

A loud cheer broke out in the room.

"All right, very good," the doctor said absently. "You'll be getting your various prescriptions in ten minutes or so." He walked over to the stereo and turned it on, then nodded and left.

The stereo played slow, sappy music that made Ed look up from the puzzle and grimace. "Whooooaaa! That music *sucks!*" he said, standing. He went over to the stereo and changed the station.

"Uh, Ed," Dexter said. "I don't think you should—"

Ed found "Knee Deep" by Funkadelic on the radio and turned up the volume.

"Ooohh, I *love* this song!" he said, brightening up. Ed began to dance and made his way over to Heather. "C'mon, dance with me!"

"I . . . I don't really dance," Heather said.

"Sure you do! Watch me!" Ed began to make some goofy moves on the floor, smiling at Heather the whole time.

The other inmates in the room began to watch him, some of them smiling. A few of them began to clap to the rhythm . . . although most of them *had* no rhythm.

"See, Heather?" Ed said. "You can do it. C'mon!"

She shrugged, then joined him, quickly catching the beat.

"Ed?" Dexter called. *"Ed* . . . I really think you should maybe sit down."

"Can't!" Ed replied. "I got the music in me!"

An old man with no teeth and wild, staring eyes, grinned as he joined them, completely off-beat, but very enthusiastic.

"That's right!" Ed cried. "You, too! Everybody! C'mon and dance!"

"Ed?" Dexter said again, worried. He had a sinking

feeling in his gut that Ed was going to get them into big trouble and make it *impossible* for them to get out of Demented Hills. But when Dexter looked over at the two security guards, he saw that they were *smiling!*

"Check out the kooks," one guard said to the other with a chuckle.

They were actually *enjoying* the dancing! They were tapping their feet to the music and nodding their heads happily. Dexter was unable to keep from smiling. Seeing the guards so relaxed gave him an idea . . . a *big* idea. He leaned over to Otis and whispered, "Watch me . . . and when I say run . . . *run.*"

Dexter got up and started dancing with the others, then danced his way over to the two security guards.

"Hey, guys, I bet you got some moves," Dexter said jovially.

"Huh?" one of the guards asked.

"C'mon, let's see what you guys got!" He danced in front of the guards, nodding, encouraging them to join in.

"Oh, I couldn't really," one guard said sheepishly, looking down at his feet.

The other smirked and said, "Yeah, I'm not a very good dancer."

Dexter grabbed their hands and started pulling them toward the middle of the room. The guards laughed, embarrassed.

"Just let yourself go, guys!" Dexter said. "Feel the *rhythm!*"

Exchanging a glance, the guards began to dance

awkwardly as Dexter led them deeper into the crowd of dancing inmates.

"*There* ya go!" Dexter cried. "Just loosen up your butts! That's it! *Dance!*"

The guards got into it, flailing their arms, swinging their hips.

Ed danced wildly from one end of the group to the other, occasionally bumping the other dancers, but not really noticing. He was too involved in the music. His braids flew around his bobbing head as he flailed his arms and kicked his legs, and—

Ed accidentally kicked one of the guards in the groin. "Uh . . . no?" Ed said as the guard doubled up, groaning in pain.

Dexter took advantage of the opportunity without missing a beat. He buried his elbow in the gut of the other guard, sending him to the floor gasping for breath.

Dexter called, "Ed! Otis! Heather! C'mon, *run!*"

Ed and Dexter each grabbed one of Otis's arms and the four of them ran from the recreation room, leaving behind a group of obliviously happy, dancing mental patients.

They ran down the corridor together. It wasn't long before they had white-uniformed attendants running after them and calling for more attendants to cut them off. They went around a corner . . . around another . . . down a stairwell . . . then down another corridor and around another corner.

They stopped for a moment, leaning against the wall to catch their breath.

"Ooooh-*wee!*" Otis said breathlessly. "I should hang out with you boys more often!"

From around the corner, they could hear the sound of footsteps running toward them . . . and getting closer *fast.*

Dexter looked around frantically for some avenue of escape . . . but there was none. He pointed to a door across the corridor from them and said, "In here!"

The four of them rushed into the room and Dexter closed the door behind them, sighing, *"Whew!"*

From behind them came a deep, gurgly, animal-like growl. They all turned around slowly . . . and saw the enormous, slobbering man whom Ed had met in the recreation room the night before.

"I-I-I think I picked a bad room," Dexter stammered.

Otis whimpered, "I . . . I think I'm gonna have to take my trousers to the cleaners."

"Just don't make any sudden moves," Heather whispered.

Ed stepped forward casually, smiling at the hulking, beast-like man. "Hey, dude . . . whassup?"

"Don't get so *close* to him, Ed!" Dexter cried.

"Don't worry," Ed said. "He's cool. Aren't ya, dude. Remember me?"

The huge, scary man smiled and nodded slightly, slobbering.

"Leave it to *you*," Dexter said, rolling his eyes, "to make friends with a vicious psychopath!"

Suddenly, Wade's voice came over the P.A. system: "Attention! Seal *all* exit doors! There is an escape attempt in progress! Seal *all* exit doors!"

They all exchanged nervous glances.

"Now how do we get outta here?" Dexter asked.

From outside the door came the sound of footsteps, voices, and jangling keys.

"Check *all* the rooms!" a voice ordered.

Dexter held his head in both hands and squealed with fear. Then he noticed two rectangular windows at the top of the opposite wall. He pointed to one and said, "Help me get that window open!"

"You can't," Heather said. "They're hermetically sealed and made of triple-thick bullet-proof glass."

Dexter scratched his head, thinking fast. He turned to the room's enormous occupant. "Uh, Mister Scary Man? Can you help us open one of those windows?"

The beast-man looked at the windows, then at Dexter. Silently, he stepped forward, hefted Dexter off the floor as if he were a rag doll, then threw him through one of the windows.

Although bullet-proof, the glass was not Dexter-proof, and shattered as he shot through it like a missile.

Ed, Otis, and Heather listened to Dexter's wild cry as it faded outside the window. In the distance, they heard a muffled *thud.* A few moments later, they heard Dexter call, "Thank you!"

Outside in the corridor, the voices were growing closer fast.

"Try this one!" one of the men said.

"They're coming!" Heather whispered. "You two better go!"

"You don't gotta tell *me* twice," Otis said. He ran

forward, jumped onto the bed and bounced through the smashed-open window.

"Ed, *hurry!*" Heather said breathlessly.

"Okay," Ed said, turning to face her. "But I just wanna tell you before I go . . . you're the nicest, prettiest psychopath I've ever met."

"Aw," she said. "You're so sweet." She leaned forward and kissed him on the cheek.

Ed turned, ran to the bed, bounced off it, and . . . dove through the *unbroken* window, shattering the glass and shooting outside the building.

Chapter 15

Outside Demented Hills, Ed, Dexter, and Otis ran along the narrow, winding road that went down the hill until they reached the street below. Across the street from them, an ice cream truck was parked at the curb in front of an ice cream warehouse with its engine idling. Dexter led Ed and Otis across the street, and the three of them got into the truck.

"Hey, *hey!*" called the ice cream man as he ran from the warehouse office toward the truck in his powder blue uniform and cap. "What are you *doing?*"

"Stealin' your truck!" Otis replied.

"Don't worry," Dexter called, "we'll bring it back!"

As Dexter drove the truck away from the curb, Ed leaned out the door and waved, shouting, "Buh-bye!"

The truck was big and unwieldy, but Dexter drove it as fast as he could. As Dexter drove, Ed inspected the console. He reached down and flipped a switch at random, and a jingly tune began to play from speakers built into the sides of the truck.

"Whoooaaa!" Ed cried. "Ice cream tunes! *Cool!*"

"Will ya turn that *off,* Ed?" Dexter said.

Seconds later, the Demented Hills van sped down the hill to the street with an attendant at the wheel and Wade in the passenger seat. The attendant stopped the van at the street and turned to Wade.

"Uh . . . left," Wade said. "Go *left!*"

The attendant turned the van left, squealing across the street in front of oncoming cars. Brakes screamed and horns honked.

The van sped off in the same direction as the ice cream truck, and not very far behind.

The Good Burger employees began to arrive for work, all of them still worried about Ed and Dexter.

Mr. Baily was behind the counter when Spatch emerged from the back, spatula in hand. Locking his hands together, Mr. Baily said, "Morning, Spatch. How goes it?"

"Grrrrrr," Spatch grumbled.

"Ah, good for you," Mr. Baily said with a nod. "Well, it's time to prepare for our customers. Make sure we've got plenty of Ed's Sauce on hand, Spatch."

With another growl, Spatch went back into the kitchen. He opened the refrigerator and removed the two pots of Ed's Sauce, setting them on the grill.

* * *

The ice cream truck careened down the street, its jolly tune playing for all to hear. As it passed, children gathered on each side of the street, running after the truck, calling, "Ice cream! Ice cream!"

In the truck, Ed rummaged through the freezers, checking out all the different kinds of ice cream inside.

"I see 'em!" Dexter shouted, looking in the rearview mirror. "They're closin' in fast! And this truck won't go any faster!"

The Demented Hills van was closing the distance between them rapidly.

"Hey, Dex," Otis said, hunching down behind the driver's seat and holding his stomach. "You better slow this truck down before I throw up."

"Look!" Ed cried. "Fudgsicles! Bomb Pops! Whoooaaa! *Drumsticks!*"

"Ed!" Dexter shouted. "This is *no* time for frozen treats!" He hunched over the steering wheel, concentrating intensely on the road as he pushed the truck to its limit. Suddenly, Dexter sat up straight and his eyes opened wide. He had an idea. "No, *wait,* Ed!" he shouted over his shoulder. "Gimme one!"

Behind the ice cream truck, the van closed in fast. The attendant clenched his teeth as he pushed the accelerator to the floor. In the passenger seat, Wade leaned forward, clutching the dashboard and glaring at the ice cream truck. He didn't want those guys to get away, because he didn't want to let Kurt Bozwell down.

Out of nowhere, a brown glop hit the windshield and smeared over the glass.

"What the heck was *that?*" Wade shouted.

The attendant said, "Uh . . . I think it was a Fudgsicle."

A glob of red hit the windshield with a *splat,* then a glob of white and brown.

The attendant turned on the windshield wipers. They made disgusting moist sounds as they smeared over the glass in long brown and red and white streaks.

"Oh, *great!*" Wade barked.

In the ice cream truck, Ed was throwing ice cream bars out the window on the passenger side, stopping only to hand some over to Dexter, who threw with one hand and steered with the other.

"Have another ice cream sandwich!" Dexter shouted as he threw one out the window.

"Hey, dudes," Ed cried, grinning, "how about a *Dreamsicle!*" He threw it out the window.

Dexter took a quick left turn down a side street, then looked in the rearview mirror. The van followed. So, he jerked the wheel to the right and shot down another street. Then he grabbed an orange Popsicle and threw it out the window, laughing.

Far ahead on the road, Mr. Wheat was busy hammering the final nail in his brand new mailbox. He stepped back and admired his handiwork, smiling proudly.

"It adds a touch of refinement to the entire street," he muttered, "if I may say so myself."

In the Demented Hills van, the attendant was beginning to panic at the wheel. The windshield was covered with a smeared rainbow of ice cream colors.

"Where are they?" he shouted. "Are they still there?"

Wade leaned out the window. "Yes! We're gaining on them again! Keep going!"

"But I can't see! I can't *seeee!*"

Up ahead, Mr. Wheat checked the red flag on his mailbox. It moved smoothly, and that made him smile again.

He heard car engines growing louder *very* quickly, and along with that, he heard the jingly sound of an ice cream truck's tune. He looked to his left . . . and saw an ice cream truck swerving back and forth along the road, heading straight for him. Behind it, a white van was doing the same . . . but with gooey, colorful smears all over its windshield.

"No, *no!*" Mr. Wheat cried, waving at the wild ice cream truck. "No, *away! Turn!* Go *away!*"

The ice cream truck whizzed by . . . but the van was obviously losing control.

In the van, the attendant screamed like a baby and slammed his foot on the brake pedal. The van swerved, tilted on its side and slid along the road, throwing sparks and making an awful sound.

Mr. Wheat stumbled backward, slapping his hands on his cheeks, eyes bulging. "No, no, no!" he cried.

Sliding on its side, the van jumped the curb, slowing down rapidly. It came to a stop . . . but not before bumping Mr. Wheat's mailbox *just* hard enough to knock it over.

Mr. Wheat's shoulders slumped and a tear trickled down his cheek as he whimpered, "Oh . . . wonderful."

In the ice cream truck, Dexter checked the rearview mirror and let out a cheer. *"Hah!* Lost 'em!"

Ed had already stopped throwing ice cream bars out the window and was preoccupied with shuffling around inside the glove compartment.

"Good," Otis said, sounding very unwell. "Now you can slow down."

"No, we *can't!*" Dexter said. "Good Burger is just about to open! We gotta get there before somebody eats that poisoned sauce!"

"Why don't we just *call* 'em?" Ed asked, removing a cellular phone from the glove compartment.

Dexter's eyes widened when he saw the phone. He reached over and grabbed it out of Ed's hand, saying, *"Gimme* that!" Clutching the steering wheel with one hand, Dexter used his thumb to turn on the phone, then punch in Good Burger's number.

At Good Burger, Mr. Baily sat behind his desk in his office, talking on the phone.

"No," he said, "nothing at all here. Not a word. Anything on your end?"

Deedee walked into his office and said, "Morning, Mr. Baily. Any sign of Ed or Dexter?"

Mr. Baily covered the phone's mouthpiece with his hand and said, "I'm on with the police now." He removed his hand and said, "Uh-huh. Well, we're really getting worried here. Could you at least—oh, wait, that's my other line. One sec." He punched a button. "Hello? Uh, yes, Mother. What? I don't know. Try squeezing it."

In the ice cream truck, Dexter exclaimed, "Dang! It's busy!"

After a long, ugly belch, Otis braced himself and said, "Better step on it, Dex."

128

Dexter stomped his foot down on the accelerator, and the ice cream truck raced down the street and around a corner, on its way to Good Burger . . .

. . . Where Mr. Baily was walking out of his office.

"Anything, Mr. Baily?" Monique asked.

"Nothing," he replied, shaking his head. "No Ed . . . no Dexter." He looked up at the clock on the wall. "Well . . . time to open." He went to the door and flipped the CLOSED sign so that it read OPEN, then unlocked the door.

Two little old ladies were waiting outside, and Mr. Baily opened the door for them. "Welcome, ladies," he said as they hobbled in.

They smiled and nodded at him as they made their way to the counter.

"Hi!" Monique said cheerfully. "Welcome to Good Burger, home of the Good Burger. May I take your order?"

The ladies looked up at the menu on the wall.

"Hmmm. What are you going to have, Eva?"

"I don't know, Elsbeth. Everything looks *so* tempting."

"Well, *I'll* have a Good Burger," Elsbeth said. "With extra sauce."

"Oh, that sounds delightful," Eva said. "I'll have the same."

Monique grabbed the microphone and said into it, "Two Good Burgers, extra sauce."

In the kitchen, Spatch growled as he stirred the bubbling sauce in its pot on the stove.

Meanwhile, the ice cream truck was taking turns at

dangerous speeds and pulling out in front of cars as it ran red lights. Dexter's face was dripping with sweat as he clutched the steering wheel.

Ed was in the back, standing next to one of the freezers, slurping on a Dreamsicle. He grabbed another Dreamsicle from the freezer and walked swayingly to the front of the truck. "Hey, Dex . . . wanna Dreamsicle?"

"Don't talk to me!" Dexter screamed. "I'm too busy scarin' the crap outta myself!"

Ed turned to Otis, who was leaning against the wall of the truck, half-sitting, still holding his stomach. "How about you?" Ed asked, offering the Dreamsicle.

Otis replied, "Not unless you want me to puke all over your pants."

At the wheel, Dexter muttered to himself, "We're almost there . . . almost there."

As Dexter raced through town in the ice cream truck, Monique handed the two little old ladies their food on a tray, saying, "Here's your order. Two Good Burgers with extra sauce."

Elsbeth carried the tray as she and Eva made their way to a booth next to a window and slid slowly into their seats. They began to unwrap their Good Burgers.

"Oh, *poo,*" Eva said. "I wanted mustard."

Elsbeth said, "Well, I believe it's right over there on the condiment shelf."

"Yes, yes," Eva said, scooting out of the booth. "I'll be right back."

As Eva hobbled over to the condiment shelf, the ice cream truck ended its last mile. Dexter spun the steering wheel and the truck's tires screeched over the pavement as it turned in to the Good Burger parking lot. Dexter brought it to a squealing stop, then shouted, "Everybody out! We've gotta get in there!"

Ed was the first out of the truck, with Dexter close behind.

"Any customer!" Dexter shouted as Ed sprinted ahead of him. "Stop 'em, Ed! They can't eat that sauce!"

Ed burst through the door and stumbled to a stop. He took a moment to look around. There were only two customers . . . two little old ladies. He almost laughed when he thought about himself and Dexter dressed up as little old ladies . . . but these were *real* little old ladies! One was seated in a booth . . . the other was standing at the condiment shelf. The one in the in the booth was slowly raising a Good Burger to her mouth. He couldn't get to her in time, so he focused on the other.

With his heart hammering against his ribs, Ed ran toward the little old lady at the condiment shelf, shouting, *"Noooooooo!"*

He tackled her to the floor.

Elsbeth dropped her burger and stared in shock at the spectacle.

Mr. Baily jogged out of his office and came out from behind the counter.

"What the . . . *Ed?"* Mr. Baily blurted. "Ed! What're you *doing?"*

"Get him off me!" Eva cried. "Please! Somebody get him *off* of me!"

Mr. Baily lifted Ed off of the old woman as Dexter burst into the restaurant, gasping for breath.

"Ed!" Dexter shouted. "You okay? What happened?"

"I knocked down this old lady!" Ed replied.

"Way to *go*, Ed!" Dexter cheered.

Mr. Baily said, "Would you two mind explaining to me why this is a *good* thing?"

Dexter hurried over to the booth where Elsbeth was sitting and snatched up her burger. *"This* is why!" he said, holding the burger before Mr. Baily. "The guys from Mondo Burger poisoned our sauce!"

Mr. Baily's mouth dropped open as he babbled, frantic and confused. "But how could they . . . and where have you . . ."

"We'll explain later, Mr. Baily," Dexter said. "Just don't let *anyone* eat any of this sauce! And call the cops!" He tossed the Good Burger aside as he said, "C'mon, Ed!"

"Where are we going?" Ed asked.

"To get us a can of Triampathol!"

"What *for?*"

"Proof!" he shouted as he ran out of the restaurant.

Ed shrugged and ran along with him.

Otis stumbled into the restaurant, wheezing for breath. He leaned back against the wall and muttered, "I need a hot Jacuzzi."

Chapter 16

Outside, Ed and Dexter crossed the street and strolled casually toward the back of Mondo Burger, then ducked behind a row of bushes. There they watched, unseen, to make sure the coast was clear.

A delivery van drove slowly in the rear of the Mondo Burger parking lot, heading toward the building.

"C'mon, let's go!" Dexter said.

They stumbled out from behind the bushes and jogged alongside the van, using it as a shield to make sure no one could see them. They stayed beside the van until it stopped right at the delivery entrance door. They watched from behind the van as a delivery woman got out and walked to the door with a clipboard in hand. She pressed a button beside the door, ringing a bell. A moment later, someone opened the door and she went inside.

Dexter looked all around, then said, "The coast is clear."

The boys went to the delivery door, and Ed reached for the button, saying, "Shall I ring?"

Dexter grabbed Ed's wrist and pulled his hand away from the bell. "No! You can't just ring the bell and say, 'Howdy-do, neighbor!' We're gonna have to *sneak* into the kitchen somehow."

"Hmmm." Ed looked around thoughtfully. "I got it! Follow me!"

With the ease of an acrobat, Ed climbed up onto the roof of the van. From there, he dove toward the building, grabbing hold of a drainpipe that ran down the wall. He climbed up the pipe to the roof, then turned and peered down at Dexter.

"C'mon up!" Ed said. "It's easy!"

"Yeah, easy for you," Dexter said. He climbed slowly and nervously onto the roof of the van, then looked warily at the drainpipe. It seemed *so* far away. He made a couple of moves to jump, but he just couldn't bring himself to do it.

The door opened and the delivery woman came out of Mondo Burger and got into the van.

"Uh-oh," Dexter muttered as the woman started the van. As the van started to pull away, Dexter closed his eyes and squealed, diving toward the pipe, arms flailing. He latched onto the pipe, dangling from it dangerously.

"All right!" Ed said. "You got it!"

"Got what? I'm swingin' from the dang pipe here!"

Dexter groaned as he began to struggle up the pipe. At the top, he pulled himself onto the roof of the building, sweating and out of breath. But when he got there, Ed was nowhere in sight. "Ed? Oh, Ed? *Ed!*"

Ed's grinning head popped out of the giant straw sticking out of the giant shake that stood next to the giant hamburger and bag of fries. "Over here!" Ed called.

"What're you doin' in that straw?" Dexter asked, hurrying over to the Mondo Meal monument.

"It's right over the kitchen! I can see it! Come up here."

"How'm I supposed to get up there?"

"You just jump on the burger, climb up the French fries, jump onto the cup, and shimmy up the straw."

Dexter sighed. "What is this, 'American Gladiators'?" Grumbling to himself the whole way, Dexter climbed clumsily up the mountainous fast food meal, then up the straw. He leaned into the straw's opening and said, "Ed? You in there?"

"Here," Ed said from inside the straw, "gimme your hand!" Ed reached out, grabbed Dexter's hand and pulled.

"No, Ed, *wait!*" Dexter cried. But Ed pulled him in, and they both tumbled down the straw, yelling.

They fell through a ceiling vent and landed in a storage bin filled with packed napkins and paper towels. Ed sat up and grinned, saying, "Again! Again! Let's do that again!"

"Will you *hush!*" Dexter snapped, looking around. They were in a dark storage closet, surrounded by cluttered shelves. "Listen, Ed. I'm goin' in the kitchen first. You stay here, count to ten, then run in there and grab a can of that chemical. Then haul butt back to Good Burger. Okay?"

Ed nodded. Dexter climbed out of the bin and left the closet silently. Hunched in the bin, Ed began to count quietly to himself: "One . . . two . . . three . . . uh, wait. One . . . toe . . . no, wait, that's not it . . ."

Mondo Burger's kitchen was very busy. Workers were preparing plenty of huge Mondo Burgers. Ground meat was churned automatically in an enormous vat. Hamburger patties rolled along on the conveyor belt, where shiny steel nozzles automatically squirted precisely the same amount of ketchup, mustard, and mayonnaise onto each patty.

Troy and Griffen stood in a corner of the kitchen, arms folded over their chests, closely watching every employee.

Dexter stepped into all the activity with a big grin and said loudly, "Heeeyyy, everybody? Whassup?"

"How'd *you* get here?" Troy barked.

"Ooooh, *look* at this fancy *kitchen!*" Dexter said, looking around at all the state-of-the-art gadgetry. "*Verrry* high tech! Momma never had a kitchen like *this.*" Dexter wandered around, touching the equipment.

"Don't *touch* anything!" Troy shouted.

"Would ya look at *this!*" Dexter said, approaching the conveyor belt. He watched as ketchup, mustard, and mayonnaise were squirted efficiently onto the hamburger patties. "How does this doohickey work?" he asked, reaching over and moving a nozzle . . . then another nozzle . . . then the third.

"No! Stop!" Troy shouted.

"Don't touch that!" Griffen cried.

The pivoted nozzles began to squirt ketchup, mustard, and mayonnaise all over the place. Gooey ropes of condiments splattered all over the employees, glopping onto their white smocks and shocked faces.

"Whoops!" Dexter exclaimed. "My bad!" He ran out of the kitchen as one of the employees turned off the condiment nozzles.

Troy and a dozen kitchen employees ran after Dexter, emptying the kitchen.

Dexter ran out from behind the counter and through the restaurant, then ducked down a hallway. He spotted a door with a sign on it that read STAIRS. As Troy and Griffen and the kitchen employees followed, Kurt appeared and joined them.

"It's that Good Burger punk, Kurt," Troy growled as they headed up the stairs.

Back in the kitchen, Ed appeared and looked around. Automated machinery slapped beef patties onto the grill, flipped them, and then dropped them back onto the grill. But when he saw there was no one around, Ed crept around silently until he spotted several cans of Triampathol.

"Gotcha!" he said, snatching one of the cans. He turned and started to run out, but he slipped in a puddle of ketchup and mustard. His feet shot up in the air and Ed landed on his butt, dropping the canister. Triampathol spilled from the can. "Uh-oh," Ed said as he sat up. He stared at the spilled chemical, then looked over at the other canisters. He scratched his head . . . and an idea lit up inside his head like a lightbulb in a dark attic.

He got up, grabbed two more canisters, and took them over to the churning vat of raw ground beef. Popping the caps off, Ed dumped the Triampathol into the vat of hamburger. Then he rushed back to the shelf, grabbed two more cans, and dumped more of the chemical into the beef . . . and more . . . and more . . .

Dexter reached the top of the stairs and burst through a door onto the roof, dwarfed by the Mondo Meal monument. He could hear Troy and the others trampling up the stairs behind him, so he ran around the giant burger and hid behind it.

Troy stumbled out the door, followed by the dozen employees. But now, he was joined by Kurt, who looked very, *very* angry.

"All right, punk!" Kurt shouted, looking around. "Game over!"

"Oh, yeah?" Dexter said, stepping out from behind the burger. "*Your* game is over, clown! Right now, *Ed* is on his way to the cops with a container of Triampathol. *Hah!*"

Kurt, Troy, and Griffen exchanged a worried look.

"You think he's telling the truth?" Griffen asked quietly.

"He's probably bluffing," Kurt muttered.

They began to close in on Dexter, who was about to

turn and run. But he froze when the door opened and Ed sauntered casually out onto the roof.

"Hey, Dex!" Ed called, grinning as he held up a canister. "Look what I got!"

Dexter's head drooped and he groaned miserably. Ed had blown it. They were *finished!*

Kurt, Troy, Griffen, and the kitchen employees all turned around and faced Ed.

"Get it!" Kurt bellowed, pointing at the canister in Ed's hand.

Ed didn't even blink as the crowd of employees rushed him like a stampeding herd of buffalo. They grabbed him, and Troy took the canister from him.

"Nice try, dudes," Kurt said. "But you mess with Kurt, you go in the grinder." The kitchen employees surrounded Ed—who was still grinning goofily—as Troy handed the canister to Kurt.

Dexter joined them. He figured there was no point in running now. They'd been defeated.

"Hey!" Kurt shouted, looking at the canister. "This can's *empty!"* He bellowed with laughter as he turned to Ed. "What an *idiot!"*

Dexter looked at Ed with disbelief. "Ed . . . you stole an *empty* can?"

Still grinning, Ed said, "It wasn't empty when I found it."

Downstairs, in the empty, automated kitchen, hamburger patties sizzled on the grill . . . and they began to grow. With bubbly glopping sounds, they puffed and bloated, grew wider and taller . . . they grew . . . and grew . . . and *grew!* Each patty grew to the size of a truck tire . . . and then they began to *explode!*

The explosions knocked the remaining cans of Triampathol from their shelf. The tops popped off the cans when they hit the floor, and Triampathol spilled everywhere.

The raw meat in the churning vat began to bulge and fatten and spill out of the vat and over the floor. It pressed against cupboards and gummed up the automated machinery. The whirring equipment began to jam. A pipe broke. And the vat of raw meat grew larger and larger.

In the front of the restaurant, customers and employees began to feel a low rumbling. Cups of soda on the booth tables began to tremble. One of them fell over.

"What's that?" one of the customers asked. "What's going *on?*"

"I don't know," another customer said. "But I'm getting *outta* here!"

The rumbling grew louder as some of the customers ran out the door, until the menu on the wall behind the counter broke loose and dropped to the floor with a terrible crash. The girl at the register jumped back and screamed at the top of her lungs.

Up on the roof, they heard the muffled scream. The rumbling and shaking was so bad, they could hardly stand up.

"The kitchen!" Kurt cried, running for the door. Troy and Griffen and the employees followed him through the door and down the stairs.

When they were gone, Ed and Dexter grinned at one another.

"Way to go, dude!" Dexter said.

"Yeah! I thought so, too!"

"C'mon, Ed . . . let's get down off this stupid roof!"

Downstairs, Kurt and Troy and Griffen raced behind the counter and headed for the kitchen as the restaurant began to fall apart around them. Chunks of plaster fell from the ceiling, and the walls began to crack. Panicked customers were running for the doors, screaming.

When he reached the kitchen door, Kurt pushed through . . . but he and the others were knocked back by a mountain of bulging, growing raw hamburger.

"We've gotta stop it!" Kurt shouted. "We've gotta get to the grill!"

"We *can't!*" Troy cried.

Giant hamburger patties exploded in the kitchen, throwing meat in all directions. Kurt and Troy and Griffen were splattered by it, *covered* in it.

"Okay," Kurt said, "out! Everybody out!"

Pursued by growing mountains of meat, they turned and ran as explosions rang out in the kitchen. Sparks flew, and smoke began to billow out of the kitchen door.

"Let's just get *outta* here!" Kurt cried as he ran for the door.

Outside, Ed and Dexter dropped to the ground after climbing down the drainpipe, then ran around to the front of the restaurant. Screaming customers were pouring out the door. The building quivered like a bowl of Jell-O as Kurt, Troy, Griffen, and a dozen white-smocked

141

kitchen employees rushed out the door covered with huge glops of raw hamburger.

Sirens sounded in the distance, rapidly growing closer.

Ed and Dexter grinned as they watched, basking in the pandemonium like two sunbathers basking in the sunlight on a tropical beach.

"Adios, Mondo Burger!" Dexter said happily.

Ed waved and called, "¡Sí! ¡Estoy feliz que la hamburguesa grande destruyó el Mondo Burger!"

Two police cars pulled into the Mondo Burger parking lot and screeched to a stop. An officer got out of each car, and Kurt approached them. As Ed and Dexter watched, Kurt talked to one of the officers animatedly, flailing his arms, waving at the restaurant and shaking his head. The other officer daringly went inside Mondo Burger.

"Shall we go help 'em out?" Dexter asked.

"Let's," Ed said.

They walked over to the officer as Kurt was saying, *"No!* You don't understand. I don't know *what* happened here, *really!"*

"Sure you do, Kurt," Dexter said. "Why don't you tell the officer you've been making your burgers *big* with the help of illegal food additives?"

Kurt shook his head frantically. "No way, bro. That's *bogus!"* He turned to the policeman, pointed at Dexter and said, "This dude's *lyin'!"*

The other officer came out of Mondo Burger carrying two Triampathol canisters. He said, "Well, why don't we just check these out and we'll *see* who's lying."

The officer Kurt had been talking to turned to him with

a grim expression. "I think you'd better come with us," he said.

"What?" Kurt asked. "Are you guys outta your *minds?*"

The officers ignored Kurt's protests and began to lead him toward one of the cars.

Dexter grinned, waved, and said, "Buh-bye! You enjoy prison, now! Y'hear?"

"Yeah!" Ed called. "And remember . . . you mess with Good Burger . . ."

Together, Ed and Dexter said, "You go in the *grinder!*"

From inside Mondo Burger, explosions continued to make great belching sounds, and puffs of smoke curled against the windowpanes.

A car pulled into the parking lot and parked awkwardly in front of the restaurant. Mr. Wheat got out and looked around frantically. "What the *devil* is going on here?" he snapped. "I wanted to come here for *lunch!*" He watched as Kurt was shoved into a police car. The officers got into their cars and began to drive away.

Kurt turned around in the backseat of the police car and looked out the window, glaring at Ed and Dexter. But his attention was quickly diverted to the roof of the Mondo Burger building.

The roof began to collapse with a great cracking sound. The gigantic burger atop the building jerked . . . then began to roll across the roof with a thunderous rumble.

"What *is* the *problem* here?" Mr. Wheat asked. He turned and saw Dexter and Ed. He saw that they were looking up at the building's roof, and tilted his head back, following their gaze. When he saw the gigantic burger tumbling off the roof, he screamed and stumbled backward, slapping his hands to his cheeks. He gawked in horror as the burger dropped onto his car, crushing it like an insect in an explosion of crushed metal and broken glass.

Mr. Wheat stood frozen in place, hands on his face, staring at his demolished car, as Dexter approached him.

"How ya doin'?" Dexter asked, reaching into his pocket. He removed a roll of cash. "Listen, here's about half the money I owe ya," he said, handing over the money.

Dazed, Mr. Wheat reached out slowly and took the cash.

"I'll have the other half by the end of the summer," Dexter said. "And you, uh . . ." He nodded toward the crushed car. "You enjoy your car, now, okay?" He turned and walked back toward Ed, grinning. "What a happy day," he said.

As Mondo Burger continued to collapse behind them, Ed and Dexter walked together back to Good Burger.

"You poured that *whole can* of stuff into their meat?" Dexter asked.

"I had to," Ed said.

"You *had* to? What do you mean?"

Ed took a deep breath, then said, "See, I knew if I took the can and tried to run, there was a good chance I'd get caught, in which case they'd have taken it away from me, so we'd have no proof they were *using* it. And then I thought, even if I *did* get the Triampathol to the proper authorities, Kurt could hire high-powered attorneys who would dispute any charges brought against him or Mondo Burger by manipulating the legal system. And with America's court system congested the way it is, it would have taken months to get any kind of a conviction against him. So, I figured the best way to handle the situation was to pour the Triampathol into the meat supply so the Mondo Burger people would, ironically, become victims of their own foul play."

Dexter looked at his friend in amazement. "You thought of all that?"

"Sure," Ed said, shrugging. "I'm not *stupid!*"

Dexter smiled, but only for a moment. As his smile faded, he turned and stopped Ed, saying, "Look . . . about that contract I had you sign." He pulled it out of his pocket. "Whatta you say we just . . . forget about it, okay?"

"What?" Ed said, looking disappointed. "You don't wanna be my partner anymore?"

"Well, no," Dexter said.

"How come?" Ed asked.

Dexter explained, "Look, we can still be partners, Ed. But the money's yours. All of it. Okay?" Dexter ripped the folded contract into shreds and let the breeze flutter them from his fingers and over the pavement.

"But . . . we're still buddies?" Ed asked.

"You *know* it!" Dexter exclaimed.

They hugged one another tightly. Ed pulled away and looked into Dexter's eyes, saying, "I just want you to know that . . . I'm really gonna miss you, Dex. A lot. But I promise you . . . you'll always be in my thoughts, and in my heart. I will never forget you, Dexter Reed. Never. Good-bye, my friend. Good-bye."

Dexter cocked his head. "But . . . I'm not *goin'* anywhere."

"Ooohhhh!" Ed said happily. *"Cool!"*

Together, they walked into Good Burger.

"Here come the heroes!" Otis shouted as they entered.

The Good Burger gang cheered and applauded as Ed and Dexter looked around, surprised. Monique rushed over to Dexter, wrapped her arms around him and gave him a big kiss.

"Ed!"

Ed turned toward the sound of the familiar voice and saw Heather hurrying toward him.

"Heather!" he shouted, opening his arms as she rushed into them. He embraced her as he asked, "How'd you get *out?"*

"I jumped through the window," Heather replied. "One of the guards tried to stop me, so I hit him with a fish." From behind her back, she produced a large fish, which she held by the tail.

"Whoooaaa!" Ed cried. "You are *quite* twisted!"

Heather looked deep into his eyes, saying, "Oh, Ed." She dropped the fish and threw her arms around him. When she tried to kiss him, Ed grabbed her arm and Judo-flipped her hard onto the floor.

"Sorry!" Ed said, wincing. "You surprised me."

She smiled up at him and said, *"Excellent* flip!"

"C'mon, people," Dexter shouted. "Let's hear it for

the man who saved Good Burger!" Dexter led the group in a chant: "Ed! Ed! Ed! Ed! Ed!"

Ed spun around, crying, "What? What? What? What? What?"

Everyone burst into laughter at Ed's confusion as Heather stood, slowly wrapped her arms around him, and gave Ed a big kiss.

About the Author

JOSEPH LOCKE is the author of ten previous novels for young readers, including *Kiss of Death* and *Game Over*. He has also written the forthcoming *Alex Mack* novel, *Hocus Pocus*. He lives with his wife Logan and their dog Tucker in northern California.